"We're two of a kind, darlin'."

His fingers curled around her hand. "We thought our world was the only one." He shook his head, his sad gaze upon her. "It isn't, you know. You're finding that out, too, my poor little Garnet."

His eyes widened, grew bright with tears.

"People like us are a dying breed. Nobody out in the real world gives a tinker's dam about us. They call us the idle rich. Only a handful of us are left even in the South. We lived in a dream . . . thought War was some kind of glorious game. But it wasn't!" His eyes grew wild, his grasp on her hand tightened painfully. "War is *hell!*"

"I saw it, Garnet. It was hell! I believe in hell now. Wasn't always sure before . . . but now I know what it must be like. . . ."

"Please, Bryce, save your strength, honey," she pleaded.

"I just want to know it was worth it," he groaned.

"Yes, it was worth it. . . ." She couldn't think about the past now. She must think of the future. When Bryce was well, he would see how she had changed. . . .

REBEL BRIDE

Jane Peart

Serenade/Saga
BOOKS
of the Zondervan Publishing House
Grand Rapids, Michigan

REBEL BRIDE
Copyright © 1985 by The Zondervan Corporation
Serenade Saga is an imprint of
The Zondervan Publishing House
1415 Lake Drive, S.E.
Grand Rapids, Michigan 49506

ISBN 0-310-46692-x

All Scripture references, unless paraphrased, are from the King
James Version of the Bible.

Edited by Anne Severance
Designed by Kim Koning

Printed in the United States of America

85 86 87 88 89 90 / 10 9 8 7 6 5 4 3 2 1

REBEL BRIDE

Mayfield, Virginia
1857

A good land flowing with milk and honey.

Exodus 3:8

Part I

CAMERON HALL

Spring, 1857

When I was a child, I spake as a child, I understood as a child, I thought as a child.

1 Corinthians 13:11

CHAPTER 1

GARNET CAMERON, cantering happily home on an April afternoon in 1857, had no idea that within the hour her life would be unalterably changed. She was aware only of the soft wind in her face, the warm Virginia sun on her back, the exhilaration of riding her favorite horse through the shadowy woods bordering Cameron Hall, the family plantation.

Jumping the fence at the edge of the pasture, she galloped under the leafy arch of elms lining the road leading to the stately white-columned mansion. The clatter of hooves on the brick drive startled three peacocks strutting on the lawn and sent them scattering, as a golden flash of flying mane streaked by them.

In front of the portico, Garnet slid from her sidesaddle and tossed the reins to the Negro stableboy who ran out from the shade of the giant lilac bushes where he had been waiting for her return. Garnet gave the chestnut mare an affectionate pat on her arched neck, then, sweeping her long skirt over one arm, ran lightly up the steps and into the house.

Just inside the cool vaulted hall, Garnet paused at the sound of voices coming from the parlor. Guiltily, she recalled that her mother was having guests for dinner and had asked her to be home early to help receive them. If the guests had already arrived, she knew she was certain to be in for a scolding.

Tiptoeing over to the gold-framed mirror, she made a quick appraisal of her appearance should she be caught before she could slip upstairs to her room, unseen. The sun slanting in from the fanlight above the front door illuminated her gold-bronze hair like a halo, sending shimmering lights onto the curls that cascaded around her shoulders. Gathering handfuls of the wayward strands that had escaped their confining snood, she tucked them back, tilting the jaunty brim of her brown velvet hat with its long, red-tipped feather.

She took a minute more to straighten the jacket of her biscuit-colored riding habit, smoothed its cinnamon velvet collar and cuffs and adjusted the creamy silk stock at her throat. Turning sideways, she admired her pleasing image.

At eighteen, Garnet could not be considered beautiful. Her features were pert rather than classical, but her coloring was vivid and her enormous eyes, fringed with thick dark lashes, were unusual—like clear topaz. She was taller than average, with a slimly rounded figure. If not the prettiest, Garnet was one of the most popular belles in Mayfield County, envied by other girls who gossiped that she was vain and an incorrigible flirt, none of which concerned her in the least.

Satisfied that she would pass inspection even if she were noticed by her mother's sharp eye, Garnet moved quietly across the hall. However, just as she reached the stairway, she heard a name spoken that always caused a strange little throb under her heart. *Malcolm. Malcolm Montrose*. They were talking about Malcolm!

With one booted foot on the bottom step, Garnet stopped to hear what was being said about him. The voice belonged to one of her twin brothers, either Rod or Stewart. They sounded so much alike she was not sure which was speaking. But if it were Malcolm they were discussing, it was worth the risk of her mother's displeasure to go in and hear for herself.

Tossing aside her gloves and riding crop, Garnet turned and hurried to the parlor. Standing in the curved arch, she surveyed the room and was relieved to see that only family was present. No guests yet.

"Hello, everyone!" she called out merrily.

All four of the room's occupants looked in her direction and all smiled fondly, even though her mother shook her head slightly and glanced at the ormolu clock on the marble mantlepiece.

Ignoring the implied reproach, Garnet cast a dimpled smile at her father and, moving toward the abundantly laden tea table, stopped at his chair to bestow a kiss on his cheek. Her tall, russet-haired brothers exchanged a knowing look, but watched indulgently as Garnet helped herself to some cake.

"Garnet, dear, you're late. The Maynards will be here very soon," her mother admonished gently.

"I know, Mama, and I'm sorry, truly I am. But I'm simply famished. Just a bite and I'll go get ready. It won't take me long to—"

"To make yourself beautiful enough to dazzle poor Francis Maynard?" teased her brother Rod.

Garnet gave an exaggerated shrug. "Oh, *Francis*," she scoffed. "It doesn't take much to dazzle *him*."

"So, missy, you can do it without half-trying, eh?" asked her other brother Stewart, raising his eyebrows.

Knowing they both treasured her, that she could do no wrong in their sight, Garnet smiled archly and nibbled on her cake.

"Now, boys!" Mrs. Cameron chided her sons. "How can I ever hope to make a proper lady of Garnet when you two laugh at everything she does? And you're every bit as bad, Douglas," she addressed her husband, trying to look severe.

Garnet, with the confidence that she was adored by her parents as their only daughter and doted upon by her brothers, laughed along with the others at her mother's mild reprimand. Then, looking at Rod and Stewart, she demanded, "So, what have you two 'double-troubles' been up to this afternoon?"

"The same as you, little gypsy," Stewart retorted. "Riding all over the countryside. We did, however, honor our dear mother's request to be home early, dressed and ready to receive our guests. A point, I might

10

suggest, that you would have been wise to make as well.''

"But we also made a call at Montclair and paid our respects to the Montroses,'' added Rod.

So they had been at Malcolm's house, thought Garnet, with a small stirring of excitement. In June, after his graduation from Harvard, Malcolm would be back at Montclair for good. How she had missed him, longed for the day when he would not be going to Massachusetts in the fall. It seemed ages since Christmas, the last time she had seen Malcolm.

His dear image flashed into her mind, all six splendid feet of him, with his dark, silky hair, deep blue eyes, his high coloring and aristocratic features. He was a few years older than the twins, which meant he was nearly six years older than Garnet and had always treated her like they did. At least, until last Christmas. . . . Last Christmas had been different, Garnet thought dreamily.

But at her brother's next statement, she was jolted rudely out of her daydreams.

"You'll never guess what news is flying at Montclair,'' Rod announced with the air of one about to spring a spectacular surprise. "Malcolm is engaged to be married.''

Garnet started upright. Gripping the delicate handle of her teacup, she heard her mother's soft voice phrase her own agonized question.

"Who is the girl?''

"A sister of one of his classmates. Rose Meredith is her name.''

The parlor seemed to spin crazily and Garnet's ears rang with the words that were reverberating in her brain. *Malcolm engaged to be married? It can't be true!* she screamed silently.

"She's the daughter of a professor, I believe,'' Stewart continued. There was a trace of amusement in his voice as he added this bit of information.

"A Northern girl, then,'' Kate Cameron said with a hint of bewilderment.

"That's what comes of sending your sons up North to school. Never did understand Clay's doing that when we

11

have the University as well as Washington College right here in Virginia," commented Judge Cameron tersely.

Garnet finally found her voice, but striving to make its tone indifferent, she asked, "Rod, how did you find out all this?"

"Apparently they had just gotten the news. Seems that it's a bit of a surprise to all of them, too. We were visiting when Bryce showed us a picture Malcolm had just sent home."

"Is she pretty?" Garnet asked sharply.

Rod turned to his twin. "I'd say so, wouldn't you?"

"If you like them dark-eyed and demure," Stewart grinned.

"She's probably a terrible 'blue-stocking'," remarked Mrs. Cameron. "Most Northern girls are."

"If you mean by that 'well-educated,' Mama, I believe Miss Meredith is, indeed. Mr. Montrose read us part of Malcolm's letter. His fiancée is 'intelligent as well as beautiful.' Those were his words, if I'm not mistaken."

Trying to conceal the effects of this news, Garnet clenched her teeth and concentrated on the contents of her teacup. If she could just manage to compose herself until she could escape to her own room, she thought desperately. She could not bear to think of attracting her mother's anxious attention or exposing herself to possible teasing by her brothers. She attempted to make her shallow breathing normal while the conversation flowed unheard around her.

Unknowingly, her mother came to her rescue. "Garnet, dear, you really must go and get ready. . . . It's getting late."

Gratefully Garnet stood up with a great show of reluctance.

"Oh, bother, I'd much rather eat supper like this . . . not have to fuss. . . ."

But even as she spoke she was moving toward the parlor door. Once out in the hallway, out of sight, she picked up her skirt and flew up the curved staircase, her little leather boots tapping on the polished steps.

Safely in her bedroom, Garnet's composure crumpled. Malcolm to marry someone else? Harsh sobs choked her as she pressed her fists against her mouth to stifle the sound. It couldn't be true! It just couldn't!

Why, she had been in love with Malcolm Montrose forever! Or at least ever since she was twelve! She had dreamed of marrying Malcolm someday—believing that he was only waiting for her to grow up. And last Christmas, at Mamie Milton's wedding, he had looked at her differently, had treated her differently and, Garnet was convinced, had thought of her differently. Her mind raced back to that day. . . .

That crisp December afternoon Oak Haven had been transformed into a winter fairyland. The gracious mansion was decorated festively for Christmas. With garlands of fresh greens entwined through the banisters of the center circular staircase and holly tied with red ribbon and suspended from the sparkling crystal chandeliers, it was an enchanting setting for a holiday wedding.

Garnet, one of the ten bridesmaids, was particularly pleased that Mamie had chosen emerald velvet for the gowns. The color set off Garnet's hair gloriously.

She recalled coming into the hall in a flurry of cold wind and drifting snowflakes. Malcolm, handsome in a dark waistcoat and ruffled shirt, was the first person she had seen. He had greeted her with hands outstretched.

"Why, Garnet, I declare you look too pretty to be real!"

Her heart had turned over with happiness. It had been almost more than she could bear to have Malcolm gaze at her like that.

After the ceremony they had danced nearly every dance together as Malcolm, in a teasing, reckless gesture, had torn up her dance card. Later, they had eaten supper on the staircase by themselves, out of the range of Garnet's ever-watchful mammy-nurse who had always accompanied her and held it as her sole purpose in life to "be sure Miss Garnet ax lak a lady and doan disgrace her mama."

When at last it was time to leave, Malcolm had slipped one of her small, white kid gloves into his sleeve, and Garnet had floated home in a daze.

Could it be possible that Malcolm had known Rose Meredith at Christmas? No! Garnet denied that possibility. Malcolm was too honorable to pretend an affection he did not feel!

"I know Malcolm cares for me! I know it!" Garnet railed against reality. "I saw something special in his eyes! I know I did!" she mourned.

But it had been months since Christmas, since Malcolm had returned to Harvard, and while she had been counting the days until summer when he would come home to Montclair and to her, it seemed Malcolm had fallen in love with someone else.

Suddenly the bedroom door opened, and Garnet heard the stern voice of Mawdee, her mammy-nurse. "What you doin' here mopin' lak dat for when dey is company downstairs waitin' fo' yo'?"

Garnet sat up quickly on the bed where she had flung herself in her first burst of bewildered grief. Keeping her head averted from Mawdee's eagle eye, she surreptitiously wiped away the telltale traces of tears. But Mawdee seemed unaware of her distress, and bustled over to the big armoire to get out Garnet's dress for the evening.

While Mawdee's back was turned, Garnet jumped off the bed and hurried over to the marble-topped washstand. She poured water into the porcelain bowl and, leaning over, splashed the refreshingly cool water onto her hot face.

Somehow she would get through this evening. Then, when she was alone again, she would think of something!

CHAPTER 2

THE EVENING SEEMED ENDLESS. During dinner Garnet, usually so animated, felt dull and listless. Several times she was conscious of her mother's anxious glances from her place at the head of the table. Kate Cameron was perfection itself in sapphire taffeta and point lace—calm, gracious, lovely. Garnet, afraid Kate might become aware that something was amiss, tried desperately to enter into the conversation.

Sitting between Stewart and Mrs. Maynard and across from the adoring Francis, Garnet could only toy with her food. Her usual healthy appetite had disappeared completely, and every bite had to be forced past the lump that kept rising in her throat at the thought of Malcolm.

Porter, the butler, gave Garnet a reproachful look as he removed her nearly untouched plate. No doubt her poor appetite would be duly discussed by him with Cora, his wife, who reigned in the kitchen and reported to Mawdee, who was Cora's sister. After that, Garnet would probably undergo questioning by Mawdee as to her reasons for not eating and be given some vile-tasting tonic to "perk" her up. That is unless she could come up with a satisfactory explanation.

She did manage to eat most of the dessert—fresh

strawberries with rich cream, served in dainty cut-glass bowls.

When the dinner hour was finally over, the rest of the evening stretched interminably ahead. She knew she would not only be expected to entertain the lovesick Francis, but probably her father would request that she play the piano for the guests, as well.

Garnet never knew how she survived. Perhaps the relentless training of her mentor, Mawdee, and the gentle example of her beautiful mother combined had unconsciously propelled her through the activities of the evening.

Every nerve in Garnet's body was strained to the breaking point throughout the lengthy good-nights as their guests departed. She stood with her parents and brothers, seeing the Maynards into their carriage and down the drive. Then, feigning a yawn, she excused herself with a kiss to each, and hurried up to the privacy of her bedroom.

Mawdee had not waited up past midnight, so as soon as Garnet got rid of Bessie, the sleepy little maid her mother was training, she could at last vent all the tumult within.

Holding on to the poster of her bed, Garnet doubled up with pain, gasping and sobbing. How could Malcolm have done this? To marry a Northern girl nobody had even heard of, nobody knew? To bring her to Montclair as his bride, and as its mistress?

From the unprimed depths of girlish passion to the present, she had yearned for the day when Malcolm would love her as she loved him. Now, she realized with a pang of total loss, that long-held dream had been swept away in a single day. She felt a helpless, sickening sense of betrayal. How could he have been so blind as not to recognize her love? A deep, strong resentment for this unknown girl—Rose Meredith—gripped Garnet, leaving her shaken and quivering as if from an unexpected, brutal blow.

"I can never be happy again!" she sobbed miserably. A life without Malcolm seemed unlivable.

Garnet could never remember a time when she had not been able, eventually, to have anything she wanted. Her

16

father had always arranged her life so that happiness was taken for granted—a new puppy when she had fallen out of the apple tree and broken her arm; a big, beautiful French doll for Christmas when her brothers went off to school, leaving her behind; a pony when she was five; a gentle mare when she was ten, and, on her sixteenth birthday, a magnificent Arabian, "Trojan Lady." In between, there had been gifts for every tear, palliatives for every hurt, imagined or real. Always, Garnet had been surrounded with love, caring, rare scolding, much spoiling.

Now, for the first time in her life, Garnet was discovering the bitter truth that there was at least one thing even her doting father could not ordain for her happiness—the man she loved!

As this realization filtered through the pain, a hard, protective shell began to form about the softness of Garnet's heart. And the sweetness of her secret love for Malcolm died a little.

If she could not have Malcolm, Garnet promised herself furiously, she would make him regret it if it were the last thing she ever did!

Garnet awoke the next morning to a roomful of spring sunshine. At first she did not remember the terrible shock she had suffered the night before. Then, as she awakened fully, remembrance came, and she felt the bewildering despair assail her once more.

Not daring to be around the house under the caring eye of her mother or the suspicious one of Mawdee, who was expert at ferreting out Garnet's best-kept secrets, she decided to go riding. On horseback, she was always happiest, clearest-headed, at her best. There she could think, plan, decide what she should do.

In the golden light of the morning, some of the tension, confusion and pent-up emotion began to ebb in the exhilaration she always felt seated on Trojan Lady. The fine horse beneath her responded to her slightest touch on the reins and moved forward with a buoyant step. Through the sun-dappled woods they went, horse and rider finding release in an easy trot along familiar bridle paths.

17

After awhile, Garnet grew calmer, the woods seeming to enfold her in its peace; the only sounds, those of hoofbeats on a carpet of pine needles. When she stopped to let Trojan Lady drink from the rushing stream midway through the woods, Garnet lifted her head and looked about. Through a curtain of lacy white dogwood, she could see the outline of the little house called Eden Cottage, and she knew she had reached the dividing line between Cameron and Montrose land.

Eden Cottage! Garnet caught her breath. Traditionally the "honeymoon house" to which Montrose men brought their brides for the first year of marriage, was the architect's model for the big house, a miniature Montclair, built on the site of the original log cabin occupied by the first settlers on their land. As she looked, Garnet was filled with renewed distress.

How often she had ridden by this very place and thought in passing that one day she would spend her honeymoon inside that charming little house—with Malcolm. Was it really possible to have dreamed such a dream? A dream with no foundation?

Again she felt that wild rush of defiance rising inside her, the irrational hatred for the clever Yankee girl who had somehow "tricked" Malcolm into becoming engaged.

Garnet's hands on the reins tightened convulsively and the startled mare jerked her head upward, shaking it and whinnying in protest at the sudden pull on her tender mouth. Garnet leaned forward to pat the horse's neck soothingly. Her anger was for Malcolm and the fiery energy of it coursed through her. She gave Lady a gentle kick with her heels and urged her forward. They splashed through the creek beside the rustic bridge and clambered up the other side and onward to the ridge of the hill. Here she had an almost unobstructed view of Montclair gleaming in the April sunshine.

Garnet dismounted and loosely tied Trojan Lady's reins to a nearby tree. Then, walking over to the edge of the little rise, she gazed down on the house, the source of all her plans and dreams.

What was it about Montclair that gave it such a magical quality? she wondered. It was not as magnificent as her own home, which had been designed by a famous English architect and embellished with elaborate formal gardens and Italian statuary. There were terraced lawns and rooms filled with fine French furniture. In contrast, Montclair, built with white oak felled and milled right on the plantation, and bricks made by their own people, had a simple dignity that was at once austere and appealing. Garnet could not even explain why she had always been drawn to it. Maybe it was because Montclair was so like Malcolm himself—a blend of surprising charm and hidden paths. Malcolm, who was sometimes thoughtful and quiet; at other times, light-hearted and laughing.

Everything about these surroundings reminded Garnet poignantly of Malcolm. She had often met him on this very same bridle path when he, too, was out riding. She remembered particularly the day before he was to leave for Harvard the first year. She had been a skinny twelve-year old; Malcolm, already a young man of eighteen. They had both dismounted and walked along the creek. Garnet even remembered the conversation.

"I wish you weren't going, Malcolm. Papa says it's nonsense to send Virginia boys up North to school."

"Well, my father feels differently. He thinks it's important for Southerners to learn how people in other parts of this country think, feel and live. Maybe it will be good for me to get out of my own little world for a time. Anyway, I'm curious."

Garnet had tossed her long tangled mane impatiently and had pushed her rosy underlip into a pout. "But I don't see why you have to go so far away. Papa says that Virginians should know their own state, their own people. Our own ways are good enough—better, Papa says. After all, you're going to live the rest of your life in Virginia anyway."

Malcolm laughed. "Well, I'll be home at Christmas and all during the summers. Besides, you'll be going away to school yourself before long, Garnet."

"No, I won't, Malcolm. Mama wanted me to go to the Academy where she and Aunt Lucy went or where my cousin Dove Arundell is going, but Papa put his foot down. He didn't want me to be away from home. So, I'm to have a tutor instead." Here Garnet had made a face. "But she's a *Yankee* from *Philadelphia!*"

"And that's a problem, is it?" Malcolm had teased. "I'll wager you'll lead her a merry chase."

And she had, Garnet recalled wryly. She could easily reduce the hapless Miss Simmons to tears, then run out of the house, get on her horse and ride off for the afternoon. She had managed to get away with it, too. Over her mother's protestations, her father had just called her "a little scamp" and pacified the governess. Garnet was his darling and he could never punish her nor deprive her of anything. He would have moved heaven and earth to make her happy.

With aching heart she remembered another conversation with Malcolm that had taken place when she was about fifteen, not yet "come out." On the evening of the Bachelors Ball, which she was considered too young to attend, Malcolm had come by Cameron Hall to ride over with Rod and Stewart. Garnet had poured out her pique about it to him while he was waiting for her brothers.

"It's always *when I'm older,*" she complained. "I'm tired of hearing it! Everything nice is going to happen *when I'm older!* Nothing *now!*"

"Garnet, that's not true. Lots of nice things happen now. Like your birthday. *That's* going to happen very soon—with presents, a party, all sorts of nice things."

"But it's my *sixteenth* birthday that *counts!*" she insisted. People are still telling me 'wait until you're older.' I don't want to wait! I want what I want *now!*"

Malcolm had looked at the young girl who no doubt would grow up to be a raving beauty.

"Listen, Garnet, the best is yet to come, believe me," he had told her very seriously. "You'll see. In another year or two you'll have so many beaux you'll be like a princess with knights riding up to your doorstep, begging your papa for your hand in marriage."

"I already know whom I want to marry," she told him tartly, looking up at him from beneath long, curving eyelashes.

"If you were six years older, I'd marry you myself," Malcolm had laughed.

"Then I wish I *were* six years older," she had

20

declared. But at that moment her older brothers had come clattering down the steps and she did not think Malcolm had heard her.

All at once the shock of his engagement, the crushing end to her long-held dream, struck her full force. Suddenly she began to sob. With all the violence of a thwarted child, Garnet cried wildly, bitterly with the hopelessness of frustrated despair.

Finally with a last shuddering sob, she dug her fists into her eyes, swallowed hard, and flung back her head.

A lifetime of having her dreams fulfilled, her wishes granted had given Garnet an unrealistic expectation, had instilled in her false confidence that such an existence would continue unabated.

Before her lay the serenely beautiful house where she had dreamed of going as Malcolm's bride. Now the man who could have made that dream real for her was marrying someone else.

From somewhere deep within Garnet came a taunting suggestion: *But you could still be mistress of Montclair.* The desire for revenge activated in Garnet a dark, devious part of her, heretofore undetected—unplumbed because there had never been anything she truly wanted that she had been unable to attain. Now, an insidious plan, seemingly simple, hovered tantalizingly before her. If she could not have the man she loved, *Malcolm*, she *could* have his brother—Bryson Montrose! What delicious irony to be already ensconced at Montclair as its potential mistress when Malcolm brought home his Yankee bride.

Suddenly what had appeared hopeless seemed within easy reach, and the seductive sweetness of revenge filled Garnet's heart with reckless excitement. She did not know that once the impossible seems obtainable, all obstacles of honesty and decency are swept away in the lust to grasp the dream.

Bryce was a direct contrast to Malcolm in both appearance and character. Ruggedly handsome, with an air of nonchalance, Bryce cared little for the knowledge gained from books. On the other hand, his older brother was a thoughtful scholar. Bryce was content to spend his days astride the horses he rode like an Arabian prince.

He possessed the careless charm, the good-natured personality, the well-bred manners expected of any Southern gentleman. He was, however, the dismay of every hopeful mother of marriageable daughters in Mayfield County, for although any of the three Montrose sons would have been considered more than eligible, Bryce seemed most unattainable. It was said he cared more for horses, dogs, and hunting than for the company of young ladies. This fact had discouraged most of the matchmaking mamas.

But thus far in her short life as a belle, Garnet Cameron had never failed to snare any beau she pleased in her butterfly net of coquettish smiles, flattery and winsomeness. Bryce might present more than the usual challenge, but Garnet had every confidence she could claim her prize in due time. With bitter relish she imagined the satisfaction she would feel at greeting Malcolm and his Yankee bride from the steps of Montclair.

Her frenzied thoughts were interrupted by the sound of rain pelting the leaves of the arching trees above. Feeling them on her face, Garnet realized that the sky had darkened and become heavy with clouds scudding across at an angry pace. A loud clap of thunder startled Trojan Lady and Garnet had to speak soothingly before the mare allowed her to mount and start back down the path heading homeward. By now, the rain was falling steadily. It wasn't the first time she had been caught in one of the April showers prevalent in this part of Virginia. They came almost without warning and, although they were of short duration, they were drenching.

By the time Garnet emerged from the woods, galloped along the meadow, cleared two fences taking a short-cut back to the stable, she was wet clear through. As she cantered into the slick cobblestone stable yard, she saw Tully, one of the grooms, saddled up and starting out, confirming her suspicion she had already been missed. Obviously, he was being sent out in search of her.

Garnet frowned. Sometimes it was a real nuisance to be the object of so much affectionate care. She had hoped to avoid her mother's reproach, but when she saw Mawdee, arms akimbo over her ample bosom, standing at the top of the stairs, she knew it was useless to escape her sharp-tongued scolding.

Garnet sneezed twice as Mawdee helped her out of her sodden riding habit.

"See there, Missy, what yo' foolishness done got yo'?" she demanded, glaring at Garnet, her wide-cheeked black face fierce with indignation. "Yo' done ketched yo' death of cold, iffen I ain't mistook!" She then turned to the little maid, Bessie, and ordered, "Yo' gal, fetch some hot water up to Miss Garnet's room direckly. Doan jest stand dere gawkin'! Get movin'!"

Within minutes Garnet was divested of her rain-soaked clothes and wrapped in a blanket until the younger maid could pour pails of boiling water into the iron tub Mawdee had placed before the bedroom fireplace. In a way, Mawdee's ministrations were soothing to Garnet's bruised emotions. After a brisk rub-down at the black woman's none-too-gentle hands, Garnet was tucked into her high poster bed, in a nightgown that had been warmed, and with a heated brick folded in flannel at her feet. Later, a hot lemon and honey drink was brought in for her to sip in the soft luxury of her fluffy pillows.

"Now, missy, yo' hab yo'sef a good rest and doan think about doin' no sech foolishness agin. I'll tell Miss Kate yo'll be havin' supper on a tray 'stead of comin' to de table dis ebenin'," Mawdee announced before waddling out of the room and leaving Garnet to the dubious comfort of her newly hatched plans.

Garnet was glad to be left alone, relieved of having to go downstairs to dinner with her family and ever-present guests. There were always guests at Cameron Hall. Usually she enjoyed the sociability of her family, its constant flow of company, but tonight she had so much to think about she needed uninterrupted time to herself.

Since Bryce had never shown the slightest romantic interest in Garnet, she knew this would have to be a carefully orchestrated campaign, executed with great finesse. Bryce was known to have resisted the charms of the prettiest girls in Mayfield. So, as the unsuspecting pawn in the game Garnet was prepared to play, this reluctance must be overcome.

Garnet heard the whisper of rustling taffeta on the

polished floor outside her bedroom door, scooted further down into her quilt and closed her eyes. She knew by the subtle wafting scent of lilac that her mother had quietly opened the door to look in on her. Garnet pretended to be asleep, and the door closed softly.

With a belated prick of a dormant conscience, Garnet realized her mother, whom she loved dearly, must never suspect the motives behind her daughter's sudden interest in Bryson Montrose.

CHAPTER 3

JUNE SUNSHINE STREAMING in Garnet's bedroom window gilded her hair with gold as she lifted the gossamer lace veil, fragile as a cobweb, delicately embroidered with an exquisite pattern of butterflies and flowers. Draping it over her head, she regarded herself with a curious detachment.

Standing behind her, Mrs. Cameron and Mawdee surveyed the effect thoughtfully.

"Of course, your hair will be worn swept up that day, dear, and the little wreath of orange blossoms will be pinned to your coronet," commented Kate, nodding. "It will be very pretty."

"Yes, *ma'am*. Prettiest bride I ever did see," Mawdee agreed.

"Is this all you wanted me to try on?" Garnet asked plaintively.

"Yes, dear, I think so. Everything else is just about completed. There is the wedding gown to hem, of course. On second thought, maybe we best check the length once more," Kate said quickly, puzzled by Garnet's lack of enthusiasm. "Mawdee, please pull that stool over so Miss Garnet can stand on it while I measure."

The engagement of their daughter to Bryce Montrose had come as much of a surprise to the Camerons as to the community as a whole. But it was Garnet's insistence on being a June bride that had bothered Kate most. She would have liked to have planned the wedding of her only daughter at a much more leisurely pace. As it was, there had not been time to have all her linens monogrammed, her silver engraved, or for a complete set of Beleek China ordered from England to arrive. Invitations to relatives and friends were rushed out, and not all had responded as yet, making it difficult to anticipate the number of guests attending the reception after the ceremony.

However, both families had been delighted by the unexpected joining of their offspring in marriage. It seemed an appropriate culmination to their long friendship.

"Two sons married within weeks of each other!" Mr. Montrose had declared when he dropped in at Cameron Hall to exchange congratulations with his neighbors. "I was barely back from Massachusetts, seeing Malcolm and his bride off to Europe, when Bryson announces that he, too, will be a bridegroom. Well, Sara and I could not be more pleased that Bryce, at least, is choosing a Southern girl for his wife—and the daughter of our dearest friends as well!" he beamed. "Sara is especially touched that Garnet has expressed the desire to be married at Montclair. Very considerate, knowing how grieved Sara was not to be able to attend Malcolm's wedding. Now she will be able to see one of her sons married properly."

Sara Montrose, injured in a riding accident years before, was a semi-invalid, rarely leaving her suite of rooms except for an annual trip to White Sulphur Springs for health treatments.

"I'd like to go riding! Is this going to take much longer?" Garnet sighed, hands on her hips, while Mawdee dragged over a stool.

"Only a few minutes, dear," Kate replied patiently as Mawdee helped Garnet into the shimmering ivory satin dress. As its voluminous skirt fell in thick folds over her hoop, Garnet stared at her reflection in the full-length mirror. . . .

My dress for my sixteenth birthday ball was white, too. A white embroidered dimity with little blue forget-me-

26

nots, she remembered, and narrow blue ribbon threaded through the shirred bodice and small puff sleeves. It had been a warm summer evening and the August moon rising like a huge, yellow balloon over the tree-tops made the lawn as bright as day. There had been a barbecue in the afternoon, then the ball. All the young men had clustered around the birthday girl, clamoring for dances. But it was Malcolm for whom Garnet saved the special dances, especially the one before supper so they could eat together on the cool veranda. She would have him all to herself at least for a little while. When he came to claim his dance, she had moved eagerly into his arms and gracefully out onto the polished floor.

She had smiled up at him and asked with pretty coquetry, "I'm sixteen today, Malcolm. Am I grown up enough for you now?"

"Garnet, you certainly look all grown-up and very beautiful. But I still see a mischievous little girl lurking behind all that lovely façade." He had looked down at her, half-serious, half-teasing.

Garnet frowned. "I wish you wouldn't always use such big words, Malcolm. I declare, seems like you're showing off!"

Malcolm threw back his head and laughed.

"That's what comes of going up North to school. You begin to talk so no one down here can understand a word you say!" Garnet pouted. "Papa was right, you know. The schools here in Virginia are every bit as fine as the ones in Massachusetts. All you learn up there is Yankee ideas and big words!"

Malcolm laughed again, the laughter sending sparkles into his usually grave eyes and little crinkles around them.

"Ah, Garnet, you're precious. Don't ever change!" he begged.

"But I want to change! I want you to think of me as a proper grown-up young lady!" she exclaimed.

"I may, some day, think of you as a young lady but never a *proper* one!" he teased. "Besides, no matter how old you become, I'll always think of you as a 'little sister'."

The music stopped and Garnet, still in the light circle of Malcolm's arms, felt helpless fury at his words. How would she ever make him see her any other way? 'Little sister,' indeed! How infuriating when she wanted him to think of her as someone with whom he could fall in love, want to marry, desire as the mother of his children!

Memories of that summer night came back to Garnet now, overwhelming her with unbearable longing. If it were only possible to bring it back, she knew what she would say to Malcolm. She would be done with all those silly games girls were taught to play. She would tell him straight out that she loved him. Garnet closed her eyes and swayed slightly and then heard her mother's voice.

"You can get down now, dear. I know you're tired with all these fittings and trying on and such, but we did have so little time to get your trousseau ready. . . ."

Garnet stepped down off the stool, knowing that it wasn't that she was tired, only heart-sick, remembering that moment last summer when she had had the chance to tell Malcolm and maybe make the difference in the destiny of each of them. What was it he had said to her?

"You have more charm than anyone has a right to have, Garnet. Too much, maybe. It won't win you any friends among the ladies, I'm afraid, and it's going to bring unhappiness to a mighty number of young men, I'd wager."

His remark had sent dancing lights into Garnet's eyes. She had wanted to say, "But it's *you* I want to charm— it's *you* I want to make happy!"

Then Francis Maynard had come to claim his dance and there had not been another opportunity for her to be alone with Malcolm. Now it was too late. Would she go her whole life long, regretting a moon-drenched night and the lost opportunity to speak of her love?

"Aren't you feeling well, Garnet?" It was again her mother's voice, soft with concern, that brought Garnet back to the present.

Garnet stared blankly at Kate and shook her head. She was remembering what her mother had said to her after she and Bryce had announced that they were engaged and wanted to be married as soon as possible. Her mother had come into her bedroom and, in her own tactful way, had questioned Garnet about the suddenness of her decision.

"If you're sure . . ." Kate had begun. "If you have

searched your heart and soul, and know beyond a doubt that you love him. We just don't want you to make a mistake. Your happiness is our primary concern. Bryce obviously adores you. But marriage is for a lifetime and you are very young. I wouldn't want you to persuade yourself that you love a man, only to find out too late it was not really love at all.''

It was as if her mother could read her thoughts, Garnet fretted, turning away from that too-perceptive gaze. Had Kate read in her eyes the stirring of an uneasy conscience?

Now, as if mesmerized, Garnet watched her mother's long, slender fingers, making the fine stitches characteristic of any properly trained Southern gentlewoman.

But how do you stop loving someone? Garnet stormed within herself. How could she stop thinking about Malcolm? How could she stop seeing his haunting smile, his thoughtful gaze every time she closed her eyes? How could she free herself when Malcolm held her heart and mind and emotions still captive?

"I can't! I've tried and I can't!" she burst out—then gasped, clapping her hand to her mouth.

At Garnet's words, Kate stopped suddenly, aghast at the tone of her daughter's voice. As she did so, she pricked her finger and a tiny spot of blood stained the white satin hem. Kate was too startled to notice. Only the superstitious Mawdee saw and seized on it as an evil omen, one more reason Garnet should not marry in such haste.

The old mammy-nurse had been stubbornly silent on the subject of Garnet's engagement and wedding plans. She, who always had plenty to say and said it boldly, was strangely mum. Garnet thought Mawdee might be upset because she was not taking the old woman with her to Montclair. When she tried to explain that the Montroses already had twenty house-servants and that she would only bring Bessie as her personal maid so as not to cause any trouble in her new household, Mawdee just shook her head. "Didn't 'spect to go wid you" was all she would say.

Garnet knew that when Mawdee wouldn't communicate, there was no way of making her. So she tried to ignore the unusual behavior. But on the morning of

Garnet's wedding, Mawdee became very vocal with her opinions.

Garnet, in camisole and pantaloons, stood holding on to the bedposts while Mawdee tugged at the lacings of her boned corselet.

"That's enough! Don't you want me to be able to breathe?" gasped Garnet. "If you lace me any tighter, I'll faint dead away during the ceremony!"

"All yo' needs to do is to say 'I do,'" mumbled Mawdee.

"What do you keep mumbling about? You'd think I was going to a funeral, not a wedding!" declared Garnet crossly. She was feeling nervous enough without her old mammy-nurse giving her more trouble.

"Jes' all dis hurryin' up of de weddin' ain' proper," Mawdee insisted. "No time to finish wid yore hope chest belongin's—no time a'tall. Iffen yore cousin Elvira ain' done lent us her weddin' dress and us hab your mama's own weddin' veil, we couldn't of had even a proper weddin' day outfit or nuthin'." Her tone was outraged indignation.

"Three months is plenty long enough for an engagement. I never heard anything so silly," retorted Garnet haughtily. "It isn't like the olden days, Mawdee. Young ladies don't have to be engaged two years like they did in Mama's day. Besides, Bryce and I wanted to be married and back from our honeymoon in New Orleans before the beginning of Fox Hunting season."

"Huntin' or no huntin' doan have nuthin' to do with bein' proper," grumbled Mawdee.

"Yes it does! Bryce *has* to ride. His father has always been Hunt Master and, if you talk about being *proper*, we wouldn't have time for a *proper* wedding trip and do all our visiting to relatives as newlywed couples are expected to do, and still be back in time to get settled at Montclair. So stop your fussing, Mawdee!"

"Jes' too much hurryin' up is all I have to say," Mawdee insisted.

Garnet whirled around with her hands on her hips and said with exasperation, "I declare, Mawdee, I should think you'd be glad and proud instead of acting so uppity. All you and Mama have talked about ever since I can remember is how important it was for me to find a suitable husband. *You* especially!" Garnet pushed out her lower lip in exact imitation of the old black woman. "'Act lak a lady, Miss Garnet,' . . . 'Doan do dis and doan do dat, Miss Garnet . . . so's yo' can ketch yo'self a husbin'!' *Now* all you can do is complain about all this *'hurryin'*. I'm eighteen—nearly nineteen. Do you want me to be an *old maid?*" she demanded.

"Some chanct of thet!" Mawdee would not relent, just lifted her fat chin higher.

"You are an old mule, Mawdee." Garnet's eyes flashed angrily. "Now that I've 'ketched' myself a fine husband from one of the best families and biggest plantations in the entire County, and good-looking and sweet-tempered besides, you're scolding me for wanting to marry him before some other girl gets him!"

In spite of herself, Mawdee's lips twitched in an effort not to smile. Instead, she pursed them primly and said loftily. "Well, mebbe I'm some surprised myself."

"Oh, Mawdee!" Garnet sighed, half in irritation, half in affection. She knew that regardless of her criticism Mawdee loved her and was feeling a sense of pride in Garnet's good match.

"Yes'm, I is sho' enuf proud. Mr. Bryce is a fine man and I is happy yo done ketched such a nice gen'leman." With that terse statement, Mawdee turned and picked up the width of ivory satin that was spread carefully on the bed, and dropped it over Garnet's head. It slithered over the tiered hoop and starched crinoline petticoats, and fell in graceful gathered scallops, each loop caught into a velvet bow all around.

"My, my!" Mawdee hummed with satisfaction as Garnet slowly pivoted before the mirror. "Nebber seen yo' look so pretty!"

The dress was becoming, Garnet had to admit, as if it had been designed to show off her figure to full advantage, her creamy shoulders and rounded bosom. But somehow no dress in her life had ever seemed less suited to her. She had no time to ponder further, however, for the bedroom room door opened just then and Kate Cameron, elegant in mauve taffeta, entered.

"What a beautiful day for a wedding!" she said as she came around to view her daughter. "And what a beautiful bride." She cupped Garnet's chin with one cool hand and smiled, quoting softly, " '*Happy is the bride the sun shines on!*' I wonder if Bryce Cameron knows what a lucky man he is!"

Lucky? Bryce? Garnet controlled a shudder. Her pursuit of Malcolm's brother had been subtle, yet relentless. He had never suspected how deliberately his ultimate surrender had been planned.

After Garnet first formed the plan of marrying Bryce Montrose, it became a kind of obsession, controlling every waking moment, motivating every action. With reckless abandon she pursued the unsuspecting Bryce, her ruthless intensity masked in charming flirtatiousness. Since spring brought a flurry of social activities for the young people of Mayfield, Garnet lost no opportunity in showering Bryce with flattering attention.

The once indifferent young man was first astonished to be the focus of the pretty and popular "belle" whom he had known all his life as his friends' "little sister," then stunned at his vulnerability to her charms. For the first time in his rather uncomplicated life, Bryce found himself confused, dazed, enamored. With every day that passed, Garnet Cameron became more and more the focal point of his existence.

His was a lost cause. By the time he finally got up the courage to talk to his father about his desire to marry Garnet and was given permission to speak to Judge Cameron, Garnet's conquest was complete.

Lucky? Garnet wondered with a small stirring of panic. Would Bryce really think himself lucky if he knew his bride was not in love with him, but with his *brother?*

"Here comes Bessie with your bouquet, dear," Mrs. Cameron said, taking the spray of white lilacs from the little maid.

Numbly Garnet took it into her clammy hands. She gave her head a small, impatient shake as Kate was adjusting her veil. She felt chilled, yet flushed and warm. She tried to swallow, but her throat was bone dry.

In sudden frightened awareness of what she was about to do, she spun around to confront her mother. "Mama, there's something I must . . ."

But Garnet never had the chance to finish, for just then there was a knock at the door and Judge Cameron's voice called to them.

"The carriage is out front, my dear. Is Garnet ready?"

"We'll be right along!" Kate replied gaily. "Come, darling, it's time to go." She smiled at her daughter.

Garnet knew she could delay no longer. The time had come. The day she had schemed for was here. All her devious plans were coming to pass. Her heart thudded heavily. She turned jerkily and, as she did, she felt something catch. Automatically she raised her free hand to her coronet. Then there was a strong tug and the sound of ripping fabric.

"Oh, my goodness, your veil!" cried Mrs. Cameron, and there was a note of distress in her voice.

Garnet looked to see anxiety in her mother's face, which Kate Cameron tried quickly to conceal. Kate, followed by Mawdee, moved swiftly to examine the damage. Garnet saw the two women exchange a glance. Their expressions, reflected in the mirror, were inscrutable, but she felt a twinge of fear.

Then her mother was saying reassuringly, "Don't worry, dear. It's only a small tear. I don't think it will show. This lace is very old and fragile and it caught on the bureau handle. It will be just fine. . . . Now we really must go, or we shall be late."

Kate hurried forward, standing at the door, waiting for Garnet to follow. But Garnet moved stiffly, feeling the weight of her heavy satin train, the stab of hairpins securing her headdress.

At the door she hesitated, as if uncertain. Again she turned toward Kate, trembling visibly. Quickly Mrs. Cameron touched her daughter's arm. "There, there, dear, it can be fixed," she assured her calmly. "It's not the end of the world, you know. Hurry now. Your father is waiting—and your bridegroom."

With a kind of despairing bravado, Garnet swept through the door, knowing it was indeed the end of the world—at least, it was the end of the dream world she had cherished for so long.

CHAPTER 4

GARNET WOULD HAVE DEARLY LOVED a European honeymoon, but Bryce had no such inclination. In fact, he would have been far happier to stay in Virginia. He had no desire to see foreign countries, deal with a strange language or unfamiliar customs. So a compromise was struck when they left by riverboat for New Orleans three days after the wedding.

Denied the delights of sightseeing in London and shopping in Paris, Garnet indulged her extravagance in the many luxurious stores of the sophisticated and fascinating city. Bryce accompanied her and waited patiently while she spent hours trying on dresses and bonnets and making decisions on her purchases. She ordered new furniture in the ornate modern style for their wing of Montclair, as well as elegant accessories.

Garnet was experiencing her first taste of being a grown-up married lady and found that part of her new life enormously satisfying.

Bryce, who was out of his element in these surroundings, allowed his vivacious bride to satisfy her whims, content only to see her happy. His compliance with her every wish intensified Garnet's sense of guilt—a guilt she ironically released through frequent outbursts of temper. Bryce, who, beneath his rugged masculinity, was shy and gentle, reacted awkwardly, bewildered by his new wife's rapid mood swings. When she snapped at him over some incidental, Garnet was just as likely to turn around and make him laugh with a bit of mimicry, an amusing observation, a witty remark.

They had only been married a few weeks when Garnet made the surprising discovery that no matter how willful she was, how easily irritated and how often cross, Bryce put up with all her faults. She had a feeling, which she failed to explore, that he loved her unconditionally and saw something in her she did not even know about herself.

For Garnet, their stay in the fascinating city with all its new sights, new people, new experiences could have lasted much longer. Away from Mawdee's stern eye and her mother's gentle but inflexible code of behavior, she found her new freedom intoxicating.

But Bryce had been away from the fields and streams and meadows of his beloved Montclair long enough. He missed his daily horseback rides, his hunting dogs and the outdoor life he lived there. He had had his fill of touring, shopping and visiting. He was anxious to go home.

On their way back to Virginia, as was the custom, they visited relatives on both sides of the family.

The Cameron kin thought Garnet had married a fine, upstanding fellow, handsome as a prince with his tall, manly build; thick, curly hair the color of dark molasses; naturally fair coloring, tanned by sun and wind to a healthy ruddiness; his eyes, blue and clear as a child.

The Montrose clan members thought Bryce's bride was as pretty as a picture, with her beautiful skin and hair, her dimples and lusciously rounded figure, her unusual topaz eyes. Both sides of the family agreed that they made a charming couple and entertained them royally, urging them to stay longer at each home. But Bryce would not delay his return to Montclair any longer.

It was different for Garnet. Returning to Virginia and her new home, the one where she had dreamed of being mistress, was a jolting let-down. Montclair was magnificent, but living there was not at all as she had imagined it would be.

Ordinarily a young woman marrying into the family of a large plantation-owner would have moved into a very complex, demanding role. But even though Sara Montrose was an invalid, still it was she who ruled from her "ivory tower." Her personal maid, Lizzie, trained expertly to relay Sara's orders to the twenty or more house servants, kept the household running smoothly. As a result there was very little for Garnet to do. She had no duties, no responsibilities, no authority.

Since its early days Montclair had developed into one of the most beautiful plantation homes along the James River. The stark simplicity of its original design lent itself well to structural changes, additions, ornamentation and enhancements that had been built through the years, ordained by its subsequent masters and mistresses.

The house had been constructed to last for centuries to shelter the dynasty the first master had envisioned would follow him. Built on an original King's Grant when this part of Virginia was still wilderness, a network of tunnels for refuge and food storage had been built underneath the superstructure of the house—a necessary precaution in time of Indian attacks. Now, of course, such a threat was a thing of the past.

For the first few days, Garnet explored the splendid mansion. On previous visits she had seen only the first floor of the three-story house—the drawing room, the parlor, the dining room, music rooms, the veranda that encircled the downstairs area. Now it was a delight to survey all the other rooms.

The newlyweds were given their choice of one of the new wings on the second floor. Garnet chose a front suite overlooking the sweeping drive. Every window in each room commanded a view of orchards, meadow and the woods banding the terraced lawns.

When the furniture Garnet had chosen in New Orleans began to arrive, along with other pieces ordered through catalogs from Northern furniture factories, she spent a few happy weeks supervising the arrangements. A bedroom, two dressing rooms, and their own sitting room were soon lavishly decorated in the elaborate style

Garnet admired. Once this was achieved, however, Garnet found time heavy on her hands. Since there was nothing to complain of in the luxurious circumstances into which she had moved, Garnet found other things with which to find fault.

The easy-going Bryce who, once back at Montclair, reverted to his old bachelor habits of rising early to be out with his horses most of the day, found it an escape from his bride's petulance, and frequently left her to her own devices. He had decided the best way was one of least resistance and habitually gave in to her in most things.

Garnet quickly acquired a defiant attitude. Ignoring the set pattern of life at Montclair, she slept late, had breakfast served in her room, then often went riding over to Cameron Hall, often choosing to stay overnight if there were guests whom she enjoyed. If Bryce minded his bride's unconventional behavior, he did not say. Mr. Montrose liked order, but prized peace more, so said nothing. If Sara was annoyed—well, no one stayed angry with Garnet for long. She was so delightful, amusing, and playful—when she wanted to be.

Within a few weeks, Garnet found herself restless and vaguely discontented. In spite of her indulgent husband and a life of luxurious ease, marriage proved to be a great disappointment. Instead of the freedom she had expected to enjoy out from under the strict rules of decorum for young girls, she discovered all sorts of restrictions imposed by society on "married ladies."

Besides forfeiting the fun, flattery and gaiety of her life as a belle with many beaux, Garnet's disenchantment was tinged with deep regret. The underlying reason for her unhappiness for which there was no remedy, was the unalterable fact that she had married the wrong man.

In her way Garnet had become very fond of Bryce. How could she help it? He was good-natured, amiable, fun-loving, and he adored her. His only fault was that he was not Malcolm.

And there was something more that Garnet had not counted on when she had forged her plan for marrying Bryce and being established at Montclair before Malcolm brought home his Yankee bride. It was the painful fact that she faced each day as she walked through the rooms of the house where Malcolm had lived most of his life, sitting at the table in the high-ceilinged dining room where he had taken his meals. All—daily reminders of the man she loved and had lost to a stranger.

When letters arrived, bearing European stamps and postmarks, Garnet felt the ache of imagining Malcolm with Rose, honeymooning in Italy. And as the October date for their return grew near, Garnet's tension increased beneath her frenetic activity.

Malcolm sent a telegram from New York, stating that he and Rose would be taking a steamboat to Norfolk, the train to Richmond, and then on to Mayfield and Montclair.

"I want the whole family here to welcome Rose when they arrive," Mr. Montrose said at dinner the night before. "Since this is her first trip South, we want to show her what real Southern hospitality is like."

His words seemed directed to Garnet, whose unexpected comings and goings were a source of irritation to a man accustomed to promptness and order in his life.

But Garnet found it impossible to comply with her father-in-law's request and rose early, slipped out and galloped through the morning mist to Cameron Hall, where she stayed until Bryce was sent to fetch her back. Even then she fussed, procrastinated, and delayed to the last possible moment meeting Rose, the reality of her own shattered dream.

Part II

MONTCLAIR

Winter, 1857

Through a glass, darkly . . .

1 Corinthians 13:12

CHAPTER 1

GARNET WAS NOT PREPARED for Rose to be so beautiful. It would have been easier for her to believe Malcolm had been drawn to his Yankee bride by her intellect. It was more painful to see that he may have been dazzled by her exquisite beauty as well.

From the glance Garnet had given her upon entering Sara's upstairs sitting room where everyone had gathered to greet the newlyweds, Garnet saw a young woman of elegance and poise. Her traveling costume must have been bought in Paris. Of sage green serge appliqued with dark green cording, both its cut and style were flawless. Rose's abundant dark hair was worn in the new French chignon. Her enormous brown eyes were heavily lashed; her features, delicate; her complexion, translucent.

It was easy to see how any young man might fall prey to such beguiling beauty, but it was galling for Garnet to meet in person the girl Malcolm had preferred to her.

Garnet's quick assessment prompted characteristic reaction on her part. With her usual dramatic flair, she covered her inner turbulence by whirling into the room, pretending a gaiety and enthusiasm she did not feel. Greeting everyone merrily, Garnet claimed the right to welcome Malcolm with a sisterly kiss, then took a place near her mother-in-law's chaise lounge, showing Rose unequivocally her prior position in Sara's affections. Too, from this vantage point she could observe Rose closely without being too obvious.

For all her gay façade, Garnet was seething. All the old wounds of unrequited love were opened at seeing Malcolm again. He was more handsome than ever, she thought with anguish. His new status and the experience of travel had given him a maturity and polish that only enhanced his dark good looks. He seemed more at ease with himself, laughed more readily, conversed with his parents with new assurance.

The conversation flowed animatedly, filled with talk of Rose and Malcolm's trip. As Garnet listened, almost ill with envy, the only thing she could find immediately to criticize about Rose was her New England accent. Rose's voice, though low and refined, still held a brisk clarity that sounded strange in a room filled with softly slurred syllables.

But Rose's replies to Sara's eager queries about Paris fashion and the plays they had seen in London were gracious and lively. And she answered Mr. Montrose's questions with intelligence and respect. Garnet could see that Rose was making a favorable impression on her new relatives.

Temporarily excluded from the conversation, Garnet took the opportunity of casting a surreptitious glance at Malcolm. When she saw him unobtrusively holding Rose's hand, a bitter resentment gripped her. Unable to cope with the glaring truth of Malcolm's choice, Garnet jumped to her feet, declaring that she must go change out of her riding habit.

"Well, young lady, don't spend too much time primping and be late for dinner tonight!" teased her father-in-law. "Tonight we celebrate Malcolm's and Rose's first night at Montclair as husband and wife."

"And I shall be going downstairs for this very special occasion," announced Sara, smiling fondly at her eldest son.

"That will make it a *real* celebration, my dear." Her husband bent over her thin hand and kissed the fingertips.

Garnet gave a little toss of her head, letting her long

reddish-gold hair swing back from her shoulders, and said with a slight edge to her voice: "Well! If tonight is to be such a special occasion, I'd better go make myself presentable!"

As she passed his chair, Bryce caught her wrist playfully and chuckled, "But, honey, you *always* look beautiful!"

"Spoken like a true Southern gentleman!" Mr. Montrose roared with laughter. "I believe marriage is taming you, my boy. You'll soon be a real poet!"

Garnet cocked her head and smiled charmingly at her father-in-law, but her eyes were on Malcolm who was looking at her with amusement.

"Marriage has strange and mystical powers to change people!" she replied archly.

"For the better, I hope!" Bryce grinned.

"That depends upon where you were when you started," Malcolm remarked enigmatically.

In the laughter that accompanied his comment, Garnet left the room, but underneath, she felt a shaft of pain.

Once in her own dressing room, Garnet pressed both hands against her mouth to stifle the dry sobs that rushed to choke her. She closed her eyes against her white-faced image reflected in the full-length mirror. She had not imagined it would be so hard. To see Malcolm again—to be in the same room with him—*and* the woman he loved!

She saw now that her childish scheme to make Malcolm regret that he had rejected her was like a knife flung in anger. It had turned, instead, to inflict deeper pain on the one who had hurled it.

Given time, Garnet might have been able to face the inevitable—that Malcolm's marriage was a *fait accompli* that could not be changed. Maybe if she had dealt with it then, she could have coped with it. But she did not have time. Just then the door to the dressing room opened, and Bessie entered, all grins and chatter.

"Oh, ma'am, isn't Mr. Malcolm's lady the purtiest little thing? She so dainty and talk so sweet! I do declare I wuz sayin' to Tilda, I doan know when I seen a lady so . . ."

Garnet whirled around furiously. The last thing she needed right now was to hear anyone singing Rose's praises. Bessie's entrance was ill-timed, and the little maid's thoughtless ramblings further fired Garnet's anger. Jealousy rose within her, obscuring everything else.

"Oh, hush up, Bessie!" she snapped. "Go fetch my hot water. I have to bathe and change for dinner. And hurry up about it, too!"

Everything vanished from Garnet's mind but outshining Rose. Determinedly she chose the most flamboyant of the extravagant gowns she had bought in New Orleans on her honeymoon. Of peacock blue peau-de-soie, the gown was designed with a fitted basque, sashed in wide grosgrain ribbons, tied in back and falling in long streamers over the flounced skirt. The Vandyke neckline revealed her gardenia-white skin.

Regarding her image with narrowed eyes, Garnet tried to picture herself as Malcolm would see her. She wished she could wear the Montrose rubies, the legendary Bride Set of pendant earrings and necklace. But, of course, as long as Sara was alive, no other Montrose wife would wear them. Instead, Garnet fastened on the pearl necklace with its coral medallion Bryce had given her as a wedding gift.

With a final pat to her coiffured hair, drawn up to show off her small, flat ears, and swirled into a figure eight in back, Garnet felt ready to go downstairs and face the events of the evening.

Even knowing she looked her best and that her spritely conversation had captured its usual appreciative audience, Garnet found to her dismay that the effort required to sustain it soon produced a pounding headache.

Sitting across the table from Malcolm was unbearable. Even though he laughed at her witticisms and bantered with her in teasing affection, it was Rose to whom his attention was drawn most often, his eyes resting upon her ardently in the softness of the candlelight.

Garnet struggled to keep her bright smile in place. It was difficult to keep herself from staring at Rose. Some inner magnet kept pulling her to the radiant face of her victorious rival. On two such occasions Rose met her glance and Garnet's face flushed. That delicate, intelligent face—those grave, penetrating eyes sent a dart of conviction into Garnet's innermost being. Could Rose

43

guess what she was thinking? Garnet wondered in consternation.

After dinner, when they were all sitting in the parlor having coffee, Garnet punished herself further by watching the touching tableau—Malcolm hovering solicitously over Rose, making sure she had her coffee with just the right amount of cream; lingering by her side even as he responded to his father's questions about England. When at length Malcolm suggested Rose might be weary after the long day of travel and the excitement of their homecoming, they said their good-nights before taking the woodland path over the bridge to Eden Cottage.

Rose came to Garnet then, both hands extended, and smiling said, "I've been looking forward so much to meeting you, Garnet. I've always wanted a sister."

Taken off guard, Garnet said the first thing that popped into her head. "How funny! I have never felt the slightest need of one!"

The moment the words were uttered, Garnet could have bitten her tongue. The expression on Rose's face was so startled, her dark eyes widening at the rebuff. Garnet was instantly penitent. But it was too late.

Bryce cast her a quick look, then immediately stepped up, saying smoothly, "Well, *I* have, Rose. Garnet's never had to share the spotlight with anyone before, so she hasn't missed having a sister. But I can't tell you how pleased I am that Malcolm's marrying you has given me one at last!"

His gallant remark removed the sting from Garnet's careless words, and some of the color that had drained out of Rose's face returned. Under Bryce's obvious admiration, she even blushed lightly.

Garnet squirmed inwardly. Bryce had never before given her such a cold, disapproving look. But it was not until later, when she was brushing her hair at her dressing table, that he stopped at the door of her dressing room and mentioned the incident.

"I think you hurt Rose's feelings tonight, honey," he began.

A look of honest contrition briefly crossed Garnet's face, but then she quickly affected an airy nonchalance.

"I say what I feel! If people get their feelings hurt . . ." She shrugged indifferently.

"Well, it's not a very charming trait, honey." Bryce's voice was gentle, but it held a note of warning. "Rose is family now. We want her to feel . . . welcome, don't we?"

Bryce came in, walked over behind her, then placing both hands on Garnet's shoulders, leaned down and kissed her cheek. "It's just that I don't want Rose to get the wrong impression of you, darling. I want everyone to love you like I do, that's all."

Garnet endured the embrace as she had all his others. Bryce was a dear and so undemanding in every way she did not want to offend him unnecessarily. So she checked the defensive words that sprang to her mind. But she stiffened and, with a half-sigh, Bryce left to go into his own dressing room.

Alone, Garnet flung down her silver-handled hairbrush. Bryce couldn't possibly understand what she was going through! How could he?

She shuddered as a cold fear clutched at her heart. If tonight was any example of what lay ahead of her, how could she endure it? To go on pretending for the rest of her life that she was happily married to one brother— when all the time she was dying of love for the other?

Pulling her velvet peignoir about her shivering shoulders, Garnet rose and went quickly into the bedroom. She wanted to be in bed, pretend to be asleep before Bryce joined her.

She was trembling as she slipped into the massive mahogany bed with its arched, ornately carved headboard. It was torture to see Malcolm with Rose, to know that at this very moment they were probably in each other's arms. She squeezed her eyes tight shut, willing herself not to weep and cry out in her desperate longing to be in Rose's place.

Garnet pounded her pillow with a clenched fist. If only she could bring back yesterday when she had ridden with Malcolm over the hills and through the woods between their two plantations, when they had laughed together, long before he had gone North to school—before there was anyone else! Before there was a Rose! *I could have made him love me! I know I could have!*

Garnet buried her face in the pillows. But now it was too late. She had ruined everything and there was no going back.

CHAPTER 2

ALTHOUGH GARNET HAD ALWAYS LOVED Christmas and looked forward to it with a child's eagerness, Christmas of 1857 promised to be quite different from any other, and she did not anticipate it with any of her usual enthusiasm.

She had discovered, however, that she was a fairly good actress and was learning to guard her words and actions lest she ever reveal her true feelings for Malcolm or her resentment of Rose. It was like walking a tight-rope daily, and the strain of it often made her cross and sullen.

Knowing she had to cope somehow, Garnet flung herself into the holiday festivities with abandon. Virginians began celebrating early in December with a round of parties, open houses, balls and gatherings of every kind, and Garnet accepted all invitations. Consequently, she was rarely at home.

Christmas morning, however, was a tradition at Montclair. Everyone rose early for the gift-giving ceremony on the front porch, where the Montrose field hands and their families assembled on the drive to receive their presents. Afterward, the Montroses went upstairs to Sara's sitting room for the family gift exchange.

A fire was glowing cheerfully in the white marble

fireplace and the room was filled with crimson hothouse roses in milk glass vases and decorated with holly and other fresh greens. Sara had her own small fancifully trimmed tree, sparkling with delicate hand-painted ornaments, cornucopias of marzipan in the shape of fruits and flowers, tiny candles in fluted tin holders.

A round table near Sara's chaise was piled high with brightly wrapped packages and everyone took a turn pinching, shaking and examining them, making exaggerated guesses as to their contents.

Mr. Montrose, in a jovial mood brought on by his feeling of benevolence and the holiday spirit, beamed at the assembled members of his family with a heightened sense of his good fortune. Even his delicate Sara seemed less languid this morning—no doubt happy to have all three sons home at the same time.

Their youngest, Leighton, called Lee, handsome in his VMI uniform, was handing his mother her coffee. He'd grown like a reed since fall. The two other boys and their wives seemed content and happy. Well they might be, he thought with pleasure, regarding his two attractive daughters-in-law.

Of course, Malcolm's Rose was the undisputed beauty, all demure charm this morning in a cherry red dress trimmed in velvet braid. And then there was Garnet, as reckless and headstrong as Bryce, so they were well-matched, and would probably in time settle down and have strong, healthy children like themselves.

Surely my cup runneth over! was Clayton's thought, which surprised him somewhat as he was not given to thinking in Scripture verse. But, indeed, he had much for which to be thankful this year.

"Who is going to play Father Christmas?" asked Sara.

"Lee should do the honors. He's the youngest and still believes in him!" joshed Bryce.

"Look who's talking! I remember someone getting up ten times on Christmas Eve to shake me awake, swearing he heard reindeer's hooves on the roof!" teased Malcolm.

"Well, whoever is going to do it, let's get on with it!" exclaimed Garnet impatiently. "Mama's expecting us at Cameron Hall at noon, remember." She was thinking of the traditional Open House and buffet held each Christmas afternoon for friends and relatives of the Camerons.

Still, Garnet was particularly anxious to see how Malcolm would react to her present for him. She had purchased it some time ago, on her honeymoon in fact, and had kept it for this special occasion. Noticing the handsome stickpin—a jade four-leaf clover set in gold—in the window of a shop in New Orleans, she had bought it on impulse.

Bryce had been puzzled by her urgency. Christmas shop in June? Personally, he had thought the tiny piece of jewelry an insignificant sort of present for his brother.

"Why not wait and get him some riding gloves or a shaving case—something useful?" he had suggested.

Of course Bryce had no idea of its secret meaning for Garnet, that it symbolized a precious memory—a day with Malcolm that lingered bittersweet and unforgettable—one she sincerely hoped this gift would recall.

She and Malcolm had gone riding together and dismounted to let their horses drink from the stream that ran by Eden Cottage. Looking for violets on the mossy bank, Malcolm suddenly dropped to his knees and, when he arose, he was holding out a four-leaf clover to Garnet.

"For good luck," he had said. "Not that anyone as pretty and clever as you needs luck!"

But Garnet had taken it gratefully, later pressed it, and had kept it in a small porcelain pillbox on her dressing table ever since. It had been a reminder of that special afternoon—the only thing Malcolm had ever given her and, therefore, priceless.

Perhaps it had meant something to him, too, Garnet had thought hopefully. Lately, she had begun to fantasize that Malcolm's spontaneous feelings for her were complicated by the fact that she was so much younger than he, that he had regarded her through the years as his friends' "little sister" and consequently suppressed any romantic inclinations toward her. But then Rose was only a year older! Garnet recalled indignantly.

She looked over at Malcolm, but he was fingering the smooth leather cover of some book Rose had just given him, touching it with appreciation and embracing Rose with his eyes.

Her moment of anticipatory happiness was gone, as swiftly and completely as if a cold wind had blown across her heart, and she felt quite miserable again.

The little gift exchange over, it was time to leave for Cameron Hall to attend the Open House. It could not have come too soon for Garnet, who had found it an unbearable burden to continue to chat and act pleased and happy over the many presents that had been showered upon her.

Downstairs, waiting for the carriages to be brought around, Garnet gazed in the mirror and adjusted the satin bow of her bonnet. In spite of her inner pique and disappointment over Malcolm's gracious but obviously non-specific thanks for his gift, Garnet looked enchanting in her dark blue pelisse trimmed in soft gray squirrel fur, her red-gold curls peeking out from under the shovel-brim of her matching blue bonnet and framed by the lighter blue satin lining.

She recalled the wizened-faced old jeweler in the shop in New Orleans squinting at her through his wire-framed spectacles.

"This is specially fine jade, madam," he had told her. "They say when you give jade, you give a part of yourself. Did you know that?"

Garnet had given Malcolm a part of herself for years—all her childish dreams, her impetuous affection, her unrivaled admiration. Then she had given him the most important part of herself—her heart.

Just at that moment, Garnet looked up and, over her shoulder, she saw reflected in the mirror Malcolm and Rose descending the staircase, hand-in-hand, and something cold and hopeless wrenched her soul.

CHAPTER 3

ALL DAY DECEMBER THIRTY-FIRST, Montclair hummed with preparations for the annual New Year's Eve party and Midnight Supper. Welcoming the new year, 1858, was to be especially festive for it was also the official reception honoring the two Montrose brides.

The house was still decorated for Christmas with a tall cedar tree in the front hall, its pungent scent mingling with the smell of its twinkling wax candles. The house servants were dressed in immaculate attire for the occasion—the men, in new blue broadcloth coats; the women, in wool dresses worn under white ruffled aprons starched so stiff that they crackled as they moved about.

Cut-glass bowls of eggnog and cranberry punch were set at either end of the long table, along with candied fruit; dark, spicy fruitcakes on milkglass pedestals, and tiered silver compotes holding nuts, sugared orange peel, and French chocolate bon-bons.

Upstairs in her dressing room, Garnet was getting ready, fighting back the cloud of depression that had threatened to descend all day. The thought of celebrating another year at Montclair filled her with dread. She had never thought being in constant contact with Malcolm and Rose would be so impossible. Suddenly she felt something stirring within her, a longing to be free, like an imprisoned bird impatiently beating its wings against the restraining cage.

Even the sight of her ball gown did not lift her dismal spirits. It was an extravagance of salmon-colored satin and tulle. Its froth circled the low, off-the-shoulder neckline and was gathered in loops all around the wide skirt, caught by silk flower nosegays. She fastened in the new coral pendant earrings Bryce had given her for Christmas that matched the medallion on her short pearl necklace.

She had heard the recurring sound of carriage wheels on the drive below as the guests arrived, and she could already hear the murmur of conversation and the sound of music drifting up from the lower floor of the house. But Garnet felt reluctant to go down. To pretend a gaiety she did not feel seemed absurd. She did not want to start a new year or look into the future. It was the past she clung to—the dream of what might have been. In that dream everything was the way it used to be. Her sorrow was that she knew she could no longer hold onto her dream; yet she hated living in a world so irrevocably changed.

Garnet walked over to the window and leaned her burning head against the frosty pane. Montclair, on this winter's night, was bathed in moonlight and glowed with a luminescent beauty. The river in the distance was like a sheet of silver. It had turned very cold since the light snow of Christmas, and icicles dangled like crystal prisms from the eaves above the windows.

Sadness suddenly overwhelmed her and, as she gazed out into the winter darkness, the lights of the lanterns set along the drive to mark the way for carriages blurred into sparkling diamonds through her tears.

She whisked them away. This sadness she felt was not new. She was experiencing it more and more often. If Garnet had tried to search her heart, she would have discovered the cause. But Garnet rarely explored her own feelings. If they frightened her, as this unexplained sadness did, she ran.

Tonight was no exception. Blocking out the heavy, smothering feeling, she rushed out of the room and down the stairs, toward the lights and the music and the laughter of the party.

The doors to both parlors had been folded back, and the floors polished for dancing. As she came down the steps, Garnet could see couples spinning like colorful tops to the newly imported European dance, "the waltz."

Garnet had been standing only for a moment on the edge of the floor, tapping her satin-clad foot to the rhythm of the tune, when she was claimed for the next set.

After that, she danced every dance. But the one dance, the special one just before midnight, she had determined to reserve for Malcolm. She knew, of course, that this dance was traditionally to be danced with one's special beau, fiancé or husband. Making the arrangements called for some clever manipulation. But Garnet was never at a loss for long. A few minutes before the midnight hour, she slipped over to the band leader and suggested he announce a "Paul Jones." This dance required two circles—the men on the outer one; the ladies moving counterclockwise in the inner circle. When the music stopped, one's partner was the person facing. Garnet agreed to give the leader a signal and, when she was opposite Malcolm, the musicians would stop playing.

Her ruse worked, and she feigned great surprise to find herself standing opposite Malcolm as the sweeping bars of the waltz began. He bowed, held out his arms, and she moved into them smoothly.

Was ever a man so romantically handsome? Garnet wondered, looking up into Malcolm's smiling blue eyes, feeling as if she could drown in their depths, longing to reach up and touch the silky waves of his dark hair. He looked so magnificent in his velvet-collared dress jacket, with the tucked, ruffled white shirt. Then she saw with delight that he was wearing the jade four-leaf clover stickpin in his gray silk cravat.

Deliriously happy, Garnet smiled radiantly, seeing her own gladness reflected in his expressive face as he guided her in the expertly executed steps of the new dance. They danced so beautifully together, with neither a hesitation nor a misstep, that people watching them took vicarious pleasure.

At the first stroke of the grandfather clock in the hall, the music stopped and people began to count the remaining seconds as they milled about, seeking that special one with whom to share the dawning of the New Year. Garnet's fingers tightened on Malcolm's.

"Oh, Malcolm!" she burst out impulsively. "Why did you ever have to go up North to school? Everything would have been so different if only . . ."

But in the current of voices, laughter, the swish of skirts and the shuffle of feet, Garnet's words drifted away. Malcolm did not even seem to have heard them. Instead, he leaned down, kissed her lightly on the cheek, saying, "Happy New Year, Garnet" and went in search of Rose.

Watching his tall figure move through the crowd, a tide of grief and despair rushed over her in a terrible, choking flood. Mindlessly, she turned and pushed her way to the French doors leading out to the veranda.

Outside, she took great gulps of the stingingly cold air, then leaned against one of the porch posts. Gradually her hot coursing blood cooled, and she shivered.

As the keen sharpness of the winter night clarified her clamorous emotions, Garnet knew if she were not to go mad she would have to quell her terrible longings, force herself to stop thinking of Malcolm. She clenched her teeth, stifling a groan. Even so, she knew the riotous emotions were still there, lingering behind every thought.

Later that night, long after Bryce was peacefully sleeping, Garnet tossed restlessly. She had fallen asleep quickly, then awakened with Malcolm's name on her lips. She sat up, her forehead beaded with perspiration, her heart pounding wildly. Had she spoken his name aloud? She glanced over at Bryce who slept on, undisturbed.

Garnet lay back upon the pillows, staring into the darkness. It was wrong, she knew, to dream of Malcolm now. Dreadfully wicked! And yet how could she help it? Seeing him every day, seeing Rose.

Rose was the problem! Rose was the root of all her unhappiness, Garnet fumed. Without Rose . . . Malcolm

54

would surely be hers. Then a cold, insidious thought crept into the heat of her turmoil. If Rose were gone . . . if Rose should die! Garnet felt the bitterness rise up in her, seeping through her like a poison. If there were no Rose, then Malcolm would be free to love her.

Bryce stirred beside her and suddenly Garnet was bathed in cold sweat. How could she be thinking these awful thoughts with her own husband lying beside her? God would surely punish her!

Garnet began to tremble. She hardly ever thought of God. Garnet was afraid of God. She did not know when the fear had taken root, but as with many things in her life that frightened or confounded her, she had simply ignored it. What disturbed her most was that God was difficult to ignore. With an effort, she now thrust away the thought of God and His justified wrath at her sinful thoughts.

Instead, Garnet's mind turned to the more tangible things she could handle. For her own survival, her own sanity, she knew she must get away from Montclair, go where she wouldn't have to see Malcolm or Rose and be consumed with envy.

Garnet woke up late the next morning. Her head ached but she felt oddly revitalized. She remembered having been awakened before dawn when Bryce rose and went into his dressing room to don his riding clothes. She had lain there in the predawn darkness of the room and thought over the events of the night before. Now she was more determined than ever to leave Montclair. She refused to stay here and eat her heart out in weakening daydreams, frustrated hopes and frightening, vengeful nightmares.

As soon as she was fully awake, she called for Bessie to send for her little trunk from the attic, and by the time Bryce returned at midday, her plans were made.

In two weeks time Garnet had left Montclair for a prolonged visit to her mother's relatives in Savannah and Charleston. And none too soon—for it was about then that Malcolm had announced proudly to the family that he and Rose were to have a child in late summer.

CHAPTER 4

WITH THE BABY JONATHAN'S BIRTH late in August, Garnet found more and more excuses to be away from Montclair. It became increasingly difficult for her to be around the shining happiness of Rose and Malcolm's unabashed pride in their son.

An incident that occurred a few months after Jonathan was born precipitated a flaming row with Bryce and sent Garnet off for a prolonged visit to some of her mother's relatives in Savannah.

It happened the day the photographer came to take pictures of Rose and the baby to send to her family in Massachusetts. The family had gathered in Sara's sitting room so she could observe the procedure. The photographer was busy arranging the pose, while the others formed an admiring circle about the adorable infant and his lovely mother.

It was Rose who seemed to notice Garnet standing to one side, largely ignored. Sweetly, she asked, "Would *you* like to hold Jonathan, Garnet?"

Startled, Garnet quickly put her hands behind her back as if afraid that Rose might thrust him into her arms. "Good heavens, no!" she exclaimed. "I wouldn't know the first thing about holding a baby!"

"No better way to learn," chuckled Mr. Montrose,

giving Bryce a sly wink, but Garnet turned away furiously.

She didn't want a baby, she thought angrily. She didn't want *Bryce's* baby. She didn't want any child if it couldn't be Malcolm's.

If Rose had been hurt by Garnet's refusal, or the others puzzled by her attitude, it was because no one knew Garnet was sick with envy. Her secret anguish drove her frustration to an unbearable pitch and afterward she provoked an unnecessary quarrel with Bryce.

The result of it was that she packed again and went off for another lengthy stay with some cousins. Since one of them was about to be married, the wedding was a convenient explanation for her abrupt departure.

During the next two years, their marriage followed this unpredictable pattern, with Garnet's impulsive comings and goings. Sometimes Bryce accompanied her, but he was never content for long away from the life of riding and hunting the land he loved. Because Bryce loved Garnet devotedly, he allowed her to come and go at will, even if he did not understand her need to do so.

At times, Garnet had bouts of conscience about Bryce. She knew she withheld the generous love due him, denied him the rapturous fulfillment that was his right, imprisoned them both in a marriage so limited that love's ideal joys and triumphs had not been attained. She also knew he loved her with all her shortcomings, her whims and weaknesses.

Most of the time they got on well, for they had much in common. Their roots were the same, and these were deeply grounded in their families and in the land. Even their sudden quarrels were quickly over and, like children or sunshine after a summer storm, they were soon laughing and teasing each other again.

It was on one of the occasions when Garnet had gone to attend a cousin's wedding near Charleston that the news of Fort Sumter's surrender reached Montclair. She came home at once to a flurry of excitement, rumors, and turbulent reaction. At Montclair, as all over Virginia, the discussion and debate was whether the state would follow South Carolina and secede from the Union.

A constant parade of neighbors, fellow planters, friends and relatives arrived and departed daily from Montclair as Clay Montrose had served in the legislature and was influential in the state as well as Mayfield. It was not at all unusual for twelve or fifteen extra people to be at the dinner table each evening, and the guest rooms were filled continually. At the table, furious and heated conversation raged over the issues of states rights, government coercion and secession. Each gentleman wrestled individually with the decision as to how he could best serve the newly formed Confederacy.

To add to the excitement Bryce's younger brother, Leighton, had left VMI to join the Army, and had moved up the date of his wedding to Garnet's cousin, Dove Arundell, so they could be married before he reported for duty.

There was no question where the Montrose sympathies lay. Their duty seemed clear—to class, to state, to country. Only Rose was caught in the sad conflict between her native state, her personal convictions, and her love for her husband. She was the single, silent witness to the tragic tearing asunder of the Union both her family and the Montrose ancestors had mutually fought to establish.

Gentlemen were rushing to form volunteer companies to defend what some hot-heads were declaring would be an imminent "invasion" by Federal forces. Everyone seemed caught up in an excess of regional patriotism and wild enthusiasm. None more than Bryce, who, along with his fellow planter-class friends, found a new channel for his inherent cavalier lifestyle.

As soon as Virginia seceded, and the newly elected Confederate President Jefferson Davis was brought to Richmond to form a cabinet, Bryce went to seek a commission, and Garnet went with him.

It might have been Paris, so gay was the city in those first months. There seemed no end to the round of parties, balls, and theater performances. The population had doubled as the men newly appointed to government and military positions, with their wives and families, flocked into Richmond.

A Cameron cousin, Nellie Perry, was one of the

leaders of Richmond society, and her gracious town-house on Franklin Street, the center of many a festive social scene.

"Oh, my dear, I'm so delighted you've come," Nellie greeted Garnet. "There's so much going on, you can't imagine. So many of our fine young men have thronged here to show loyalty to our noble President and support our Cause. Many from as far away as Georgia and Louisiana. And so much entertaining to be done. You'll be a real help."

Garnet could not have been happier to help in such an endeavor. She relished the excitement, thrived on the activity, gloried in the gaiety. Here, she could escape the melancholy that haunted her days at Montclair, avoid the reminders of the love she had lost.

Cousin Nellie's parlor was the scene of many fun-filled evenings, and no soldier in gray Confederate uniform was considered a stranger there. Nellie relied on her pretty cousin to welcome each of them warmly and to instigate much of the impromptu entertainment. There was plenty of food and music, with gray-coated soldiers gathering around the piano to sing such songs as "Bonnie Blue Flag" and "Dixie," and always the popular game of Charades in which Garnet with her gift for mimicry outshone all the rest.

When Bryce received his captain's commission with no delay and went to a nearby camp to train, Garnet stayed on at Cousin Nellie's. Almost every afternoon they went out by carriage to watch the drilling and parading at the camps, as if these were social events. The soldiers themselves were jubilant and bragged that one Confederate could lick twenty Yankees. It was a carnival atmosphere, and Garnet reveled in it all.

At last Bryce's training was finished and they returned to Montclair for him to say his farewells, do his final packing, and select the horses he would take with him to his regiment, along with one of the Montrose black men who would serve as his bodyservant.

"But you must come back here, Garnet," Cousin Nellie insisted. "I don't know what I'd do now without you!"

"Of course," Garnet agreed happily, inwardly thanking her cousin for giving her the perfect excuse to leave Montclair. With so much fun and frivolity in Richmond, Garnet had no intention of sitting out the war in the dull, back roads of Mayfield.

At Montclair, she had Bessie scurrying and sewing, readying a wardrobe to take back with her. She would need more ball gowns and bonnets to compete with some of the ladies now making the social scene in Richmond. President Jefferson's attractive wife, Varina, had joined him in the spacious executive mansion, which had become the center of social life. Garnet felt sure, that with Cousin Nellie's standing in the community, they would be invited to some of the fêtes and receptions there.

If she had not been so preoccupied with herself, Garnet would have observed some of the obvious changes the War was bringing to Montclair. She might have observed Malcolm's subdued demeanor in contrast to Bryce's buoyancy in his new role as a Confederate warrior. If she had been more sensitive, she might have noticed that Rose's vibrant coloring had paled, that those wonderful dark eyes had lost their laughter.

But Garnet was far away—in a world of her own creation. So an incident with Bryce on the day before he was to join his regiment came as a mild shock.

Entering the bedroom where he was packing, she noticed a small, black leather book lying near a pile of freshly ironed shirts.

"What in the world is *this?*" she asked, for Bryce was not a reader.

"Rose's 'going-away' gift to me," Bryce grinned. "Said I should carry it in the pocket right over my heart. Maybe she thinks it will protect me from a stray Yankee bullet. I hear they can't shoot worth a hang."

"What is it?"

Bryce held it up so she could read the title.

"*The New Testament?* Surely Rose doesn't think *you're* a true believer like *she* is!" Garnet demanded.

Bryce raised his eyebrows. "And how do you know I'm not?" he countered.

Garnet flounced away, tossing her head indifferently,

but Bryce's voice followed her. "For that matter, Garnet, what do you know about me at all?"

The strange question hung between them in a room suddenly tingling with tension. Her hand was on the doorknob and Garnet did not turn around nor answer, but went out of the room without saying more.

Since Garnet never let anything troublesome bother her long, she soon dismissed the unusual exchange with Bryce. She did not want to think deep thoughts or ponder religious sentiments as Rose did, and she felt a bit annoyed that Rose should have given Bryce such a gift.

Their small storm passed, and Bryce seemed his usual high-spirited self the day he left Montclair. The whole family stood on the porch to see him off, and Garnet felt immensely proud of her young husband, handsome in his new uniform. As he galloped up with his special dashing skill on his thoroughbred horse and waved his hat in farewell, the sun glinted on his tawny hair.

It was entirely different, however, on the day Malcolm left. For days a queer oppression hovered over the house—even Garnet felt it.

Not wishing to tell him goodbye in front of the others, Garnet had gone into the garden where she could watch from behind the high pivot hedge until she saw his man, Joseph, bring the horses around to the front of the veranda.

Her heart thudded heavily when she saw Malcolm's tall figure, looking dignified and splendid in his new Confederate uniform. He seemed to hesitate as if considering reentering the house. Then he smoothed his dark hair in a characteristic gesture, donned his wide-brimmed hat, and walked slowly down the steps. Joseph held Crusader's head while Malcolm mounted, then started at a brisk canter down the drive.

As he came near the place where Garnet was secreted behind the hedge, she dashed out. "Malcolm! Malcolm!" she called.

He turned his head and, seeing her, smiled and reined in Crusader. Joseph, on the other horse, halted at a respectful distance.

"Garnet! I missed saying goodbye to you. Wondered

61

where you were. I thought maybe you'd gone over to Cameron Hall.''

"No!" she reached up and stroked Crusader's neck. "I just didn't want to tell you goodbye in front of everybody.''

She looked up at him, memorizing every feature of that well-loved face, all at once aware it might be a long time before she saw him again. All the old aching anxiety she used to feel each fall when he left for Harvard assailed her. "The worst thing is I don't have anything . . . I mean, I didn't know what to give you as a farewell gift. . . .'' she finished, shrugging, feeling the sting of tears in her eyes. She blinked and turned away, so that Malcolm wouldn't see them.

But he leaned down and touched her cheek. "Look, Garnet,'' he said gently, and unfastened the two top buttons of his tunic, opening it to show her pinned inside the jade stickpin she had given him for Christmas two years before. "My good-luck talisman.''

Overwhelmed, Garnet tried to speak, but her throat was too tight. A blazing joy rushed through her at the thought that Malcolm would be keeping that small "part of herself'' with him, perhaps carrying it into battle. But her joy was short-lived, for his next words reminded her poignantly of the reality of their situation.

"I must go, Garnet. Comfort Rose if you can and be kind to her and little Jonathan.''

Nearly blinded by tears, speechless with the wounding impact of his words, all Garnet could do was nod. Malcolm clicked to his horse, and Crusader moved forward.

As she watched him ride away, Garnet wanted to scream, "Come back, Malcolm! Come back!''

At the gate she saw him turn in his saddle, look back and lift his hat in a waving salute. Then he cantered through the gates and was gone.

For some reason, at just that moment Garnet glanced up at the house and thought she saw a shadowy figure standing at the window of the downstairs master bedroom in the wing Malcolm shared with Rose. With a little clutching sensation, Garnet wondered if Rose had seen her talking with Malcolm and if she minded that Garnet's had been the last farewell.

Garnet shrugged and walked back into the garden. What difference did it make one way or the other? Malcolm belonged to Rose in a way he could never belong to her. All she had of Malcolm were memories of by-gone days.

Suddenly she remembered Malcolm's parting words: "Comfort Rose if you can, and be kind to her and little Jonathan."

Garnet gave her head a careless toss as if casting off such tiresome requests. Rose and Jonathan were not *her* responsibility! And she had no intention of taking them on, in spite of what Malcolm had asked. Besides, there were plenty of servants to care for Jonathan, and Rose seemed content enough with her Bible reading and piano playing and walks in the woods. It was not any concern of *hers*, Garnet assured herself.

"I have enough to do just taking care of myself!"

CHAPTER 5

BACK IN RICHMOND Garnet was again caught up in the social whirl at Cousin Nellie's. There was an open house every day, and her relative's home soon became a mecca of the popular young people now in Richmond. The house rang with the sound of young voices and laughter and running feet up and down the polished circular staircase.

Among the throngs of people from all over the South crowding into the Confederate capital were many from Maryland who preferred to be refugees rather than live under Yankee rule. Among them were the beautiful Hetty Cary, who quickly became the most sought-after young lady in Richmond. Accompanying her was her vivacious cousin, Connie.

Garnet also circulated with this attractive group of belles and officers making the rounds of parties, balls, theater, and late suppers. She had never been happier. Sometimes, in rare moments, she would suddenly think how odd that all this was going on while, just a few miles away, men were preparing for war. But these were only fleeting thoughts, for the war was still unreal and Garnet lived for the moment.

And *this* was her moment. She had recaptured that brief season before her precipitous marriage when she had basked in flattery and flirtatious attention. Even her married status seemed to add a bit of allure for the admiring young soldiers who frequented Cousin Nellie's parlor.

Leave was easy to obtain that summer, and Bryce was often at the house on Franklin Street, enjoying seeing Garnet surrounded by fellow officers, and realizing he wnet
that they go down to Montclair when he was away from camp, but she always found a reason to put it off. There was always a party to attend or an evening of "tableaux" that she was directing.

As it turned out, they did not find time to go home to Montclair that summer, and then quite suddenly Bryce did not come nor was he heard from for a few days. Even Garnet sensed a creeping anxiety as rumors of a tremendous battle to be waged at Manassas spread throughout Richmond. She knew Bryce's regiment, attached to General Beauregard, was there.

During the battle, special prayer services were held in all the Richmond churches. Because everyone else was going, and because it was expected of the wife of an officer, Garnet went too. But she was most uncomfortable, feeling herself strangely detached from the kneeling, prayerful women around her.

The deep, melodious voice of the minister called the people to pray with David from the Psalms. There was a rustle all about her as desperate wives and children of the men even now engaged in battle flipped through their Bibles to find the right place. Garnet, who did not own a Bible, sighed impatiently until Cousin Nellie held hers so that Garnet could read along with her: "God is our refuge and strength, a very present help in trouble. Therefore we will not fear. . . ."

But suddenly Garnet was seized with fear, real and quivering throughout her body.

The church seemed unbearably close as the service proceeded. Garnet moved, shifting her position, but she was wedged in between Cousin Nellie's voluminous skirt and another lady whose head bowed devoutly, sat stiffly immobile.

With one finger, Garnet loosened the ribbons of her

bonnet, for she was finding it difficult to breathe easily. Then her bodice seemed too tight, her stays cutting sharply into her waist. Her mouth felt dry, and she could not swallow. When her heart began to flutter, and she felt suddenly faint, she sought out the possible exits, her eyes darting feverishly from side to side. If only she had found a seat in the back of the church instead of marching up front to the Perrys' pew. Panic gripped her at the realization that she was trapped here until the end of the interminable service.

She would have stood up, in spite of everything, and rushed out right then, except that the minister began to address the congregation, and she could not go without causing a commotion. She clenched her hands tightly in her lap, and tried to listen.

"There is not one here who does not have a son, brother, husband, friend, or relative in the fray. . . ."

The names flashed like fire across her mind: *Malcolm! Rod and Stewart! Bryce! Maybe even Leighton!* All the men in her life, and those she had met so casually in the last few weeks. All of them were there, in danger— killing, or perhaps, being killed!

Garnet's throat tightened, and she felt as though she were being strangled. How could she sit here another minute and be reminded of all she could lose. Hadn't she lost quite enough already?

Then everyone was standing to sing the final hymn: "The Lord is my light and my salvation, whom shall I fear?"

The words rang in her ears: "To sing praises unto Thy name and of Thy truth in the night season . . ."

The night season! Surely this was the darkest moment she had experienced in her life thus far. What if Malcolm should be killed? Or her brothers, or Bryce?

Now everyone was kneeling and Garnet slipped to her knees, too. She was trembling. Again the voice of the minister flowed over her—as if he were speaking directly to her.

"For God hath not given us a spirit of fear, but of power and of love and of a sound mind. . . ."

As the words penetrated Garnet's clouded mind, she felt calmer. Slowly her breathing returned to normal, and the panic subsided. *Of course,* she thought, *there is nothing to fear. They'll be all right. How silly of me to be frightened!*

She did not realize, because she was unfamiliar with spiritual things, that she had been touched by the Word of God, and something within her had responded to that touch. The assurance came, startling her with its intensity, that Bryce was all right. He was safe!

Without being conscious of its significance, Garnet slipped to her knees and breathed an inner 'thank you.' Then she took a long breath and rose to join her clear, strong voice to the final hymn, "Now Thank We All Our God."

Two days later came the news of the Confederate victory at Manassas, and the city celebrated.

A victory party was in full swing at Cousin Nellie's house when Bryce appeared, his arm in a sling from a slight flesh wound. He was hailed as a conquering hero; for once, Garnet preened with pride in her husband, content to bask in the reflected glow of his glory.

Garnet did not want to miss the gaiety of the holidays in Richmond, so agreed to go down to Montclair in early December with Bryce to spend a little time with his family. While they were visiting, a bizarre incident occurred, which left Garnet shaken and uncertain.

Unexpectedly a small party of Yankees on a foraging mission had ridden into Montclair. There had already been a few reports of such intrusions in the county, but the surprising element was that the officer in charge had once been a beau of Rose's. She had entertained him, deftly distracting him from his duties as commanding officer and enabling Bryce to escape detection. Afterward, Rose had shown Garnet the secret room off Jonathan's nursery where she had hidden Bryce.

They were discussing this event one night in their bedroom at Cousin Nell's Richmond home while dressing for a Christmas party.

"Fancy, Rose being so clever," Garnet remarked.

"Yes, she was the cool one, I'll say that!" Bryce agreed. "I'd be spending Christmas in some Yankee prison right now if she hadn't used her wits."

"Or her *wiles*," muttered Garnet under her breath, unwilling to give Rose too much credit, even if she *had* practically saved Bryce's life. "I wonder just how well she knew that Yankee officer," she mused.

"Well, Rose is beautiful as well as intelligent. I would say any man, Southerner or Northerner, could well be smitten by her charms."

"Yes, I'm sure," Garnet cut him off. Rose was not her favorite subject, even though she had begun to have a grudging admiration for the girl. Curiosity, as well. Unknown to anyone else, Garnet had slipped back downstairs and listened outside the parlor door while Rose was playing hostess to her Yankee friend, and had overheard a surprising conversation.

"I had to tell you, Rose, that I have always loved you—that I love you still. I do not mean to offend you by telling you, but Fate has brought us together and will just as swiftly part us, and we may never meet again."

Garnet felt ashamed that she had eavesdropped on such an intimate conversation. Her only purpose in listening had been to catch any hint that the house might be searched.

That tender scene, however, remained etched in her memory. *Fate*, the Yankee major had called it. Probably considered it an *unkind* fate that Rose and Malcolm had ever met! In that, she and the Yankee major had something in common, Garnet thought with a resigned sigh.

"Are you ready?" Bryce's question startled Garnet out of her reverie. He was holding her cape for her, eager to be off. It would be a gala evening, for even though the reality of the War and its probable length had finally set in, Richmond was still humming with festive activity.

"Wait 'til I get my hood and muff," Garnet replied, then peered out the window. "What wretched weather! Will this rain never stop?"

"As long as it keeps McClellan bogged down on the other side of the river, it's fine with me!" Bryce gave a wry laugh.

After the disastrous defeat of the Northern troops at Manassas, the South had braced itself for a retaliatory attack all through the fall. It had not come, for the winter rains had turned Virginia roads into quagmires. With what the North considered discretion and the South called cowardice, the Union forces under General Mc-Clellan were encamped across the Potomac, preparing a spring offensive. In the meantime, Richmond hummed with the festivity of the season and of the reprieve from the fighting that had been granted by inclement conditions.

Garnet and Bryce were on their way to the kind of party that had become *très chic* in wartime Richmond. "Contribution Suppers" were gay, light-hearted affairs to which each guest brought whatever they could contribute to the meal, masking the fact that food was becoming a costly commodity. But these days, under the surface, a trace of sadness ran like a dark thread, for many had already suffered loss. Virtually no family had been left untouched. No matter how they tried to forget, everyone knew that less than a hundred miles from the city lay the enemy, poised to strike.

Garnet fought the melancholy with animation, making even more effort to sparkle and shine in the company of others. And everywhere she and Bryce went that season, Garnet was a refreshing reminder of life.

Tonight had been no exception. In fact, Garnet had been more devastating than ever. Later in their bedroom at Cousin Nell's, she had tried to hold on to the light-heartedness of the evening. Pirouetting in the center of the room, she whirled her wide skirts gaily.

"Oh, Bryce, wasn't that fun? It doesn't even seem as if there's a war going on at all, does it? I love it here in Richmond. Do you think we could live here after the War's over? Or maybe have a small house where we could give parties and such?"

Bryce shrugged. "I don't know, honey. That's a long way off. I'm beginning to agree with Malcolm that this might be a long war."

"Oh, we'll send those old Yankees packing for good before long, won't we?"

Bryce looked at her for a long moment, sighed. Under his scrutiny, Garnet felt a small pang of fear.

"But we're winning, aren't we?" she demanded, willing him to reassure her.

"I'm afraid we're outnumbered, honey," he said laconically.

"Oh, fiddle!" she retorted. "One Southerner's worth a dozen Yankees!"

"But we have to be realistic, Garnet. The Union forces have more of everything—men, guns, supplies."

"Let's not talk about things like that tonight, Bryce," Garnet interrupted him petulantly. "Let's try to be happy while we can."

Bryce crossed the room, drew her close to him in the circle of his arms, then suggested with a smile. "Let's not talk at all."

There was only a moment's hesitation before Garnet raised her arms to his neck and returned his embrace.

"I missed you," he whispered.

"I missed you, too," Garnet answered, realizing with some astonishment that it was true. Of all the attention, the admiring glances she had received lately, only Bryce knew her beyond the pretty face, the spritely manner. Except for her parents, only Bryce loved her just the way she was. With him, she never had to pretend to be nicer, kinder or anything more than she was.

His mouth on hers beseeched her to love him, its pressure awakening an ardor she had almost forgotten, and she responded with surprising warmth. Maybe she didn't love Bryce with the girlish passion she had lavished on her dream of Malcolm, but there was something deep, true and real in what she felt for Bryce.

And that night they found a tenderness in their relationship that was new, enhanced perhaps by the drama, the uncertainty, the urgency of time running out.

Afterward, held securely in Bryce's strong arms, Garnet fell asleep, her earlier fears stilled for the moment.

In the cold gray dawn of the next morning, Bryce made his preparations to return to camp. When he could get leave again or be able to come to her, neither of them knew as they said goodbye.

Bryce held Garnet close, kissed her again, and before he left, asked, "You will go down to Montclair soon, won't you, darlin'? I hate to think of Mama and Rose

70

alone so much of the time with Father away on government assignment. It would cheer them up to see you. Promise?''

"Yes, yes, I promise!" Garnet tried to hide her impatience. The last thing she wanted to do was go to Montclair, hear Sara's dreary complaints, see Rose's bravery in spite of the fact her brother was now in the Union Army fighting against her husband. "I will. I'll go right after President Davis's inauguration. And the ball, of course! You wouldn't want me to miss that, would you? Then I can tell your mother and Rose all about it. That should cheer them up!" she finished complacently.

CHAPTER 6

ON A BLUSTERY WIND-SWEPT MARCH DAY, Garnet took the
train from Richmond to Mayfield. The scene at the depot
had depressed her dreadfully. Clumps of Confederate
troops waiting for transport were standing in the drizzle
in shabby, ill-fitting uniforms, looking gaunt, cold, and
miserable. It had been a far cry from scenes in this same
place last spring and summer, when throngs of pretty
girls and cheering crowds had seen their sons, husbands,
and fiancés off to battles they were confident of winning.

Garnet huddled in the corner of the seat in the dirty,
smelly car and pressed her face against the window,
looking out onto the bleak landscape, trying to forget the
haunted looks in the eyes of those soldiers. She shivered
and drew her cloak closer, then tucked her hands deeper
into her fur muff. What lay behind was gloomy, but she
dreaded more what lay ahead of her—at Montclair!

The Montrose carriage met her at the Mayfield station.
Mordecai, the head coachman, was there to greet her
and, despite the abysmal weather, managed to look
dignified as he swept a bow before her that bared his
grizzled gray head to the pouring rain. Garnet noticed
that even his swallow-tailed blue livery looked shiny and
worn.

After seeing to Garnet's luggage, Mordecai opened the

carriage door for her and they started the trip to Montclair. The winter rains had done their damage, and the ride was bumpy and slow as the carriage wheels stuck and slid in the muddy ruts.

Starting up the long, winding drive from the gate to the house, Garnet was reminded of all the times she had ridden her horse or been driven by carriage along this same route—sometimes with happy anticipation; at other times, with a leaden heart. For instance, nearly four years ago, she had come here as a bride. With a strange sense of irony, Garnet recalled the bitter-sweetness of that day. She had won Bryce and become the future mistress of Montclair only to realize how empty that victory seemed now in the light of everything that had happened since.

As they rounded the last bend, Montclair came into view. In the gray veil of rain that almost obscured it, the great house still had an austere beauty, the slanted roof outlined majestically against the dark, clouded sky. The welcoming arms, steps that had been added when Sara had come there as a bride seemed less welcoming today, Garnet thought, and she noticed that all the windows were shuttered. It gave her a strange, foreboding feeling.

The carriage door opened, and she stepped out into the driving rain to Mordecai's mumbled apology that he had no umbrella. Running quickly up the steps, Garnet sought the shelter of the veranda and almost immediately the front door opened, and there stood Rose.

The slight girl seemed thinner than Garnet remembered, but her eyes were luminous, her face radiant as if from some inner joy.

"Oh, Garnet, how wonderful to see you! Mama has been so anxious to learn when you would be arriving that I could hardly get her to take a rest. Come into the parlor first and warm yourself. You must be chilled to the bone from your long ride."

Bessie had come scurrying forward to greet her and helped Garnet off with her sodden cape.

Shivering, Garnet followed Rose into the parlor, kicked off her wet slippers, and sank down on the rug in front of the fireplace, holding out her hands to its warmth. She began to chatter mindlessly to cover her sudden awkwardness in finding Rose in such distressed circumstances. It struck her forcefully that, while she had been enjoying herself in Richmond, this girl—only a year older than she—had been shouldering all the responsibilities of the household, an invalid mother-in-law, and a small child.

"Have you heard from Malcolm lately?" she blurted, and was surprised to see Rose blush.

"Yes, as a matter of fact, just today." A smile touched Rose's sweetly curved mouth. "He's with General Lee in western Virginia. He wasn't able to get leave at Christmas. Jonathan was terribly disappointed, of course."

Garnet turned away, unable to look at Rose's glowing face. Didn't Rose know that General Lee's men were suffering severely in the bitter mountain cold, where supplies were not able to reach them due to heavy snows? She bit her lip. Maybe, isolated as Montclair was, Rose had not heard all the news.

Garnet was saved from the necessity for more conversation by the sound of a child's voice, and a minute later, Jonathan, accompanied by his nurse, Linny, came to the doorway. At once he broke away and ran into the room, throwing himself into Rose's arms. From that haven, he peeked at Garnet mischievously.

"Say hello to your Aunt Garnet, Jonathan," Rose instructed softly, cuddling her small son.

"'Lo, Auntie 'Net," Jonathan lisped.

How like Malcolm he was! Garnet thought. The same dark, silky curls, the same high coloring.

"'Scuse me, Miz Rose," Linny interrupted, "but Miz Sara's awake and axin' who's downstairs. I done tole her it wuz Mis Garnet, an' she wants to see her rat away."

"We better go right up, Garnet. Mama's been waiting to hear all the Richmond gossip!" Rose gathered up her skirts and took Jonathan's hand.

Garnet stood, too, and started out of the room with them. At the stairway, Jonathan held out his other chubby little hand to her, and, as she took it, Garnet felt a curious sense of belonging.

"Did you know Dove is expecting?" Rose asked as they made their way up the stairs.

"No!" Garnet exclaimed, unconsciously wincing.

Rose had a child—now Dove and Leighton would have one. She knew Bryce would love to have a son. She had seen him playing with Jonathan, carrying him on his shoulders, tossing him into the air.

Garnet resisted the thought. She couldn't imagine herself a mother!

When they reached the top of the steps and turned to go toward Sara's suite, Garnet whispered to Rose, "However is she managing without Lizzie? And where in the world do you think Lizzie disappeared to? Gone over to the Yankees, most probably! Lots of Richmond families have had their slaves slip across the line to the North." She shrugged. "They say even Mrs. Jefferson Davis has had trouble keeping help."

"Well, your Bessie is helping out, and Carrie, too," was Rose's reply as she stared straight ahead.

For some reason Garnet felt she should not ask any more about it. She knew Sara was difficult, and Rose probably had had her hands full trying to keep her pacified. Lizzie, Sara's maid, had been with her for years before she so mysteriously disappeared.

Garnet spent the next hour regaling Sara with tidbits of gossip, humorous recitals of stories, social events, descriptive personality profiles of some of the people now in the upper echelon of government and society in Richmond who gathered at Cousin Nell's. She deliberately circumvented all the dreary details that Richmond society was beginning to experience as grim witness to the real cost of war. But the truth lay behind her bright words.

Sara, who had once been a social butterfly herself years ago before her accident, was engrossed in the animated reports. She leaned forward, listening to each word, her languid pose temporarily forgotten.

"And what is Mrs. Davis like?" she asked eagerly.

"Very handsome," Garnet replied. "Tall, graceful, strong features, yet there is a softness about her. I think it's her eyes, which are dark and rather almond-shaped. Her gown for the Inaugural Ball was elegant—white, with a deep lace bertha. She wore a jade brooch, leaf-shaped, a large pearl in its center. She has lovely dark hair and usually wears a flower tucked into her chignon. That night, it was a white rose."

Mrs. Montrose insisted Garnet have dinner on a tray with her while Rose went to the Nursery to eat with Jonathan. Garnet was grateful when at last Sara lay back on her pillows, looking wan and exhausted from all the vicarious excitement and said reluctantly, "Perhaps you best wait 'til tomorrow to tell me more."

Rose came in with Carrie to administer Sara's nightly dose of laudanum, then both of them left while Carrie settled Mrs. Montrose for the night.

Garnet herself felt fatigued. The dismal train trip, the jolting carriage ride over the rutted country roads to Montclair, the long draining visit with Sara combined to leave her weary.

She stifled a yawn, then asking Rose's pardon, said she thought she would go to bed early and get a good night's rest. Rose agreed graciously, telling Garnet she still had to read to Jonathan and ready him for bed.

On her way up the lovely winding stairway to her room on the second floor, Garnet passed all the portraits of former Brides of Montclair. The three current ones— herself, Rose, and Dove—were not yet among them. Rose's portrait was completed, but not framed and hung. Although arrangements had been made for Garnet's portrait to be painted, she had never had the patience to sit, and kept breaking her appointments with the Richmond artist commissioned to do the work. Dove, having married Leighton at the outbreak of the War last April, had not even made plans for her portrait. The War, thought Garnet sadly, had changed everything.

Even Montclair! Garnet was glad she would be leaving within the next day or two. Montclair was no longer the way she remembered it—the once-beautiful house now seemed empty, lonely, full of shadows.

She would be relieved to be back in Richmond where things were lively, happy, bright in spite of everything! In Richmond, there was no time to brood or worry or feel afraid, for there were always handsome officers to cheer up, flirt with, talk to. . . . Yes, thank goodness, she would soon be going back!

As Garnet prepared for bed she felt a strange restlessness, despite her physical weariness. She drew the curtains against the night and the eerie shadows cast by huge trees bowing in a macabre dance from the winter wind.

She called for Bessie to put fresh logs on the fire in her bedroom fireplace, yet still felt chilled. Downstairs, the house was quiet, but filled with unsettling noises. Garnet kept thinking how lonely Montclair seemed after the frenetic activity of Richmond.

"This place is like a tomb!" she said aloud. "How can Rose stand it?" And she huddled, shivering, under the feather quilt.

But Garnet could not go to sleep right away and lay there, listening to the wind moaning at the windows and whistling down the chimney. When she finally drifted off to sleep, it was shallow and filled with troubling dreams.

Garnet woke up with a violent start, a dreadful sense of foreboding trembling though her. She did not know how long she had slept nor what had awakened her. She sat up, tensed, stiffly alert, straining to listen. From somewhere in another part of the house she heard noises, disturbing ones that sent fear shivering throughout her body.

Then she heard the screams, terrifying cries penetrating the thick walls of the house, reaching into her secluded wing. She threw back the covers, her bare feet scarcely touching the carpeted floor as she rushed in her nightgown out from her bedroom, through the adjoining sitting room and flung open the door leading to the upstairs hallway.

At once her nostrils flared with the unmistakable acrid smell of smoke. The sound of running footsteps along the polished floors downstairs mingled with the shrieks and frantic cries.

Garnet ran to the balcony that encircled the first floor and leaned over in time to see billows of smoke and the red-orange flames leaping from Rose's wing of the house.

The house was on fire! Montclair was burning!

Part III

MONTCLAIR

Fall, 1862

But I have put away childish things . . .

1 Corinthians 13:11

CHAPTER 1

GARNET PUSHED OPEN THE GATE of the spiked black iron
fence encircling the Montrose family burial grounds. It
gave a protesting creak as she stepped inside and closed
it behind her. A brisk wind, rising suddenly, sent a flutter
of golden leaves from the branches of slender maple trees
surrounding the graveyard, scattering a profusion of
color over the newest granite marker. A banner of
September sunlight slanted across its surface, illuminat-
ing the finely cut inscription:

ROSE MEREDITH MONTROSE
1839-1862
Beloved Wife of Malcolm
Mother of Jonathan
"Love Is As Strong As Death"

Malcolm had arranged with a stonecutter in Richmond
for Rose's memorial headstone, but it had taken months
for his order to be filled, placed according to his express
directions. It was Garnet who had to see to its placement
only a few weeks ago—long after Malcolm returned to
his regiment.

So much had happened in the five months since Rose
had lost her life in the tragic fire that had destroyed one
wing of Montclair. Yet, standing in the warm fall

sunshine, it still seemed impossible that Rose could be dead. So young—a girl only a year older than herself!

Quickly Garnet placed the bouquet of late roses from the Montclair gardens on Rose's tomb, then turned and left the little enclosure. Rose was dead. Malcolm gone back to his Army duties, and Garnet left with the responsibility of their little son.

She walked over to where she had tethered her horse, Trojan Lady, and mounted. Today she was riding over to Cameron Hall to see her parents, a visit she had both anticipated and dreaded. It was always a shock to see her father. Since his stroke, Judge Cameron was pitifully changed.

Garnet started down the familiar bridle path along the creek, her heart heavy with all the newly acquired sadness. Seeing Rose's gravestone brought back all the trauma of the tragedy—a multiple tragedy, as it turned out. On the very night of the fire at Montclair, Garnet's brother Stewart lay dying of typhoid in a Richmond hospital, and, following his death, her father had been stricken.

"Love is as strong as death. . . ." The words of Rose's epitaph, chosen by Malcolm, had surprised Garnet, taken as they were from Scripture. What had Malcolm meant by these words? She knew that he was not a declared Christian even if Rose was. Garnet frowned. She hoped he had not gone all religious with some kind of imagined guilt over Rose's death.

Garnet's old fear of God had come back with fierce intensity, compounded by Stewart's death and her father's illness. How could an all-loving, all-caring God, such as Rose had believed in so fervently, do such things to people?

Garnet gave Trojan Lady a little kick and, with a flick of the reins, gave the mare her head. Then she leaned into the forward surge of the horse's gait, feeling the rush of wind in her face. She did not want to think of things like death or dying—certainly not on a gorgeous day like this! Such carefree moments were too rare for her now.

It seemed every day brought some new responsibility—like the arrival of a Montrose cousin, Harmony Chance and her little girl, refugees from a Yankee occupation of Winchester. It appeared the two would be guests at Montclair for the duration of the War.

Characteristically, Garnet felt the hot surge of rebellion against the Fate that had suddenly thrust all these people, all these odious tasks upon her. Her life of leisure and languor were over.

Leaving the woods, Garnet followed the low stone wall into the meadow that bordered the drive leading up to Cameron Hall. She took the fence easily, then slowed to an easy canter.

As the gracious white-columned house came into view, Garnet gazed on it with a fondness one sometimes felt for childhood things. Cameron Hall did seem like that to her now. Something of that long-ago time, when her life had been all sunshine and no shadows.

As she neared the house, she saw her mother in the side yard where part of the formal gardens had been converted into a vegetable garden. Garnet pulled to a stop, dismounted, and led her horse over to graze under the shade of one of the giant elms.

Seeing her daughter, Kate Cameron waved, adjusted the wide-brimmed straw hat she wore to shield her delicate complexion from the ravages of the sun, picked up an oak chip basket of carrots, and paused to pluck a late-blooming yellow rose to tuck into her belt.

The two women embraced, then stood a moment looking into each other's eyes. The unspoken message passing between them was too deep for words. A moment later, her mother's pale, compressed lips curved into a smile and she slipped her arm through Garnet's and they walked up to the house together.

"How's Papa?" Garnet asked.

"Some better today, I do believe," her mother answered. "He's resting just now. Mawdee's sitting with him. Before you go, you can look in on him. If he's awake, he'll want to see you. In the meantime we can have tea out on the porch. It's so nice and sunny—real Indian summer. I'll go tell Minna."

While her mother was inside, Garnet thought how different life was for Kate Cameron now. With her husband's stroke and her son's death, Kate's previously sheltered life had taken a tragic twist. In spite of it, she had somehow maintained her quiet dignity, her graceful bearing. And now, Garnet noticed, a new finely honed strength had emerged.

Rose had possessed it, too. Something elusive, but evident. What was it? Garnet puzzled. And how did one go about getting it?

A sullen-faced black woman came out on the porch just then, carrying a tea tray. Garnet remembered her as a kitchen helper to their cook. She mumbled something inaudible and went back in the house.

Kate shook her head slightly and sighed. "I declare, the servants are getting so difficult these days. The news of Abraham Lincoln's Emancipation Proclamation must have got through to them somehow. . . ." Her voice trailed off wearily as she dragged the rocker into the sun and sat down, a thoughtful expression on her face. "Not that I wouldn't be glad to see the end of slavery," she said, her sweet, gray eyes darkening. "I was raised with slaves, married a slave-owner, and my own father gave me ten slaves to bring with me to Virginia as part of my dowry. But my earliest recollection of its evil came when I was a child of five or six, perhaps. And the powerful impression was one of pity for the Negroes and a deep desire to do all I could to help them."

"But, Mama, you do!" exclaimed Garnet, disturbed by her mother's sad countenance. "There are no people better treated than ours here at Cameron Hall!"

"Yes, I know, but I have ever felt the guilt of it as a moral burden—lain awake nights wondering if it were impossible for a slave-owner to win heaven. I believe, if the truth were known, all Southern women are, at heart, abolitionists."

Then, as if with an effort, Mrs. Cameron changed the subject. "Well, how are things at Montclair?" she asked brightly.

Garnet made a wry face. "I guess they could be worse, but I don't see how. I would have welcomed some help and support from any number of women, but Harmony is such a ninny! No help at all!" Garnet complained.

Kate gave her daughter a look of silent reproach and said quietly, "Harmony is bearing up as well as she can under the strain. After all, she is without husband, home, and all she's been used to. We cannot expect others always to be as brave or strong as we ourselves try to be.''

Garnet accepted her mother's gentle rebuke without further comment.

"And have you heard from Malcolm?" Kate asked with concern. "I think so often of that dear little orphan boy."

"Jonathan is *not* an orphan, Mama. Malcolm's not dead!"

"I should have said *motherless*. Such a tragedy!" Kate shook her head. "And Bryce? What news is there from Bryce, dear?"

"Not much. Bryce never was much of a letter-writer. But I expect he'll get home when he can. It's Leighton we're wondering about."

Kate's face brightened. "Why, yes, I almost forgot. We got a letter from Dove and she plans to come and bring the baby soon. Here, let me read you part of her letter. . ." and Kate drew an envelope from her pocket.

"Dear Cousin Kate," she began and although Garnet listened with half an ear to the rambling description of Dove's baby girl's growth and progress, her mind wandered back to the wedding day of Dove and Leighton at Montclair in the first month of the War they all thought would be short and victorious for the South. Young men like Lee and Bryce had gone off as if on a kind of gallant adventure surrounded by an aura of romance. And no more were all those elements present than at the magical wedding at Montclair.

Garnet recalled the romantic atmosphere that day, how she had been caught up in its magic, secretly envying the mutual love she saw in Dove's radiant face uplifted to Lee's rapt adoration. For a moment she was stabbed with the stunning truth that she had never experienced that kind of love. The unexpected tears that followed she easily pretended came from the patriotic reaction to the playing of "Dixie" after the ceremony.

"So, they should be here within the month," Kate concluded, and Garnet returned to the present, knowing that she had missed most of the content of Dove's letter. "I think she should probably stay at Montclair, don't you, Garnet? I'm not sure it would be good for your father to have an infant here. Everything . . . even small things . . . seem to upset him now."

The shadows on the lawn were lengthening and Garnet stood reluctantly to leave. So much awaited her at Montclair—so much to be done. "I really must go now, Mama. But I'd like to see Papa first."

Standing at the doorway of the downstairs parlor that had been converted into a bedroom, Garnet felt the familiar constriction in her chest. How drastically changed her father appeared. The shrunken figure in the bed bore scant resemblance to the man who had once stood proudly erect, overseeing the affairs of his world with authority and vigor.

Seeing Garnet, Mawdee left her post at his bedside and lumbered over to hug her "Little Missy." Garnet leaned against the comforting bosom, wishing she could turn back time and become a child again—smothered by the love and pampering that had always been her lot until now.

When she hugged her mother goodbye, Garnet blinked back tears and left quickly, running down the veranda steps to where she had tied Trojan Lady, she swung gracefully into the saddle and turned the horse's head in the direction of Montclair, to where her new life, her new responsibilities lay. She turned several times as she moved slowly down the drive to wave back at the slim figure of Kate, standing on the shadowed porch.

With a shake of her head, as if to clear it of its shroud of memories, Garnet snapped the reins. Her carefree childhood was in the past. She must face with courage whatever lay ahead.

CHAPTER 2

AFTERWARD, WHEN GARNET THOUGHT of the year 1863, all the memories blurred mercifully into a parade of passing impressions. The winter was bitterly cold, but what was suffered at Montclair seemed insignificant when they heard of the cruel conditions under which most of the Confederate soldiers were fighting. With all their men in daily danger, the women could scarcely complain. They knew it was the same all over the South, and so learned to cope with their reduced circumstances.

With shortages of all kinds, Garnet and her little family became ingenious at finding substitutes for ordinary staples. Candles were in short supply, so they burned wood knots, split into manageable lengths and stored in baskets by the hearth. The fire kindled by the knots gave too flickering a light for reading or sewing, but cast a cheerful glow throughout the high-ceilinged rooms.

In the area of cooking they were hard-pressed to discover adequate substitutes. Soda for use in baking bread was made from corncobs, burned in a clean-swept place, and the ash gathered into jugs, then doled out a teaspoonful at a time. Tea was made from dried berries of all kinds; okra seeds, roasted and brewed, were the best and came nearer the flavor of coffee than anything else. Berries and weeds were also used for dyes, and they had even become shoemakers when leather became practically unobtainable.

Garnet found it was easy enough to be cheerful about shortages and substitutes. Those things seemed simple in comparison to her other heavy obligations. Never patient, Garnet chafed in the role of head of the household. A household of women, unaccustomed to hardship. A household of small children as well as childlike servants who never did anything unless specifically told to do so—and who often had to be shown how!

Sara was left to the tender ministrations of Dove, who was sweetness itself. Dove read to her by the hour or played cribbage with her to divert the older woman from her constant worrying.

Garnet had come to rely on Dove and to see in her cousin some of the same strengths and sweetness of character Rose had possessed. Loving Rose had come late, but now Garnet cherished and valued her memory. Harmony was a different matter—Harmony, of the mournful sighs and dire predictions.

Harmony just missed being beautiful, and one never knew exactly why. She had ivory skin, light blue eyes, hair like golden wheat. Perhaps it was the vacuity of her smile, the emptiness in her eyes, which sparkled only when they rested on Alair, her fairylike daughter.

But even Harmony could have been endured if Garnet had not begun to feel a horrible depression. She covered it well. No one would have guessed that, as the days wore on, she felt helpless and fearful much of the time. Yet something within her stubbornly refused to submit to defeat, and she continued as the leader on whom they all depended.

Garnet, who rarely in her healthy, young life had suffered from insomnia, now knew sleepless nights. One night, after lying awake for hours, counting the strokes of the grandfather clock downstairs, she got up. Shivering with cold, she wrapped herself in a shawl and huddled near the fireplace, stirring the embers of the dying fire.

She knew why she couldn't sleep tonight. Thoughts of the Montrose men, all in the front lines of duty, marched through her head—Bryce, now attached to General Stonewall Jackson's cavalry; Malcolm, still with Lee;

Leighton, with Johnson. What if they were all killed? What if none of them came home to Montclair? What then?

She shuddered and could not stop shaking. The dark room filled her with terror. Shortage or no, she would light candles, chase away the frightening darkness.

Rising, she groped along the shelf beside the fireplace for the box of candles she had kept there to use sparingly. As she did, she knocked something to the floor, and stooped to pick it up. It was a book of some kind. Her hand felt the roughness of the leather. When Garnet returned to the light of the fire, she could see that its cover was blistered and charred.

Rose's Bible! Linny had rescued it on the night of the fire, and later given it to Garnet. It was from this very Bible that Garnet had read to Rose the last day of her life.

Garnet lit a candle with shaky hands, then slowly examined the book. Almost reluctantly Garnet opened the pages, leaning closer to the firelight to better see the words. Unconsciously Garnet's eyes roamed the passages as if searching for something. She remembered what she had read to Rose now—the Twenty-Third Psalm. Even she recognized that one. She had heard it often enough at church services in Richmond. The minister had read it at Rose's funeral, as well: "Yea, though I walk through the valley of the shadow of Death, I will fear no evil: for thou art with me; thy rod and thy staff, they comfort me . . ."

I wish I believed that. Garnet anguished. *I wish I were not afraid.* But there was so much to be afraid of, so much to fear, so much evil. The safe, secure world Garnet had always known had become a frightening place.

So many people were depending on her to be strong— and she knew she wasn't! She continued to read, stopping here and there to examine passages that Rose had underlined. One passage caught her attention—"I can do all things through Christ which strengtheneth me."

Her lips moved, forming the words, murmuring them out loud, the sound of her own voice comforting. Maybe she had stumbled on Rose's secret, her inner strength. *Through Christ*—not on her own, but *through Christ, I can do all things.*

Without being aware of what she was doing, Garnet knelt beside the chair and began to pray haltingly to a God she had always feared. Unexpectedly, a soothing warmth that had nothing to do with the sputtering fire spread through her, suffusing her with peace.

After that, every day, she found comfort in repeating that simple phrase over and over, especially in times of frustration or stress. And at night, she began to read regularly from Rose's Bible until she fell asleep. At length she was able to sleep more soundly, wake more rested, feel better able to handle the crises that arose daily.

And though Garnet was unaware of the change, the others noticed a softening, a sweetness, an inner radiance that caused her, more and more, to resemble the lovely woman who had been Malcolm's wife, Jonathan's mother.

CHAPTER 3

WAR OR NO WAR. spring came to Montclair in its usual blaze of beauty. The children became as frisky as the new lambs in the pasture and the small heifers leaping through the high meadow grass. Acres of yellow jonquils and purple iris spread a tapestry of color around the house.

After the fierce winter, the balmy weather was welcome. Even the adults spent more and more time outside after the long months of confinement.

Spring slid into summer, almost unnoticed. If it had not been for letters from Cousin Nellie and the regular, if sometimes tardy, delivery of newspapers, those at Montclair might never have known a war was being waged.

Garnet would never forget the day they had all gone out to the peach orchard to pick fruit for canning. The July sun was hot, and the children were running barefoot under the trees while the others stood on ladders, plucking the fruit from the heavily laden branches.

Alair and Jonathan were playing hide and seek, with Druscilla toddling after the older children on her fat little legs, laughing her gurgly baby laugh as she tried in vain to catch up with them. The sight of them sitting in the grass, eating the ripe, juicy fruit, their chubby hands stained, their moist smiling mouths, the sunshine creating little auras of light around each small head, would often come to her afterwards. Garnet would see it bright, clear, vivid, as a treasured picture of the last day they had all been so happy.

Later, when they went into the house, Garnet found one of the Negro men from Cameron Hall with a message from her mother. Its contents sent a sliver of fear like an icy finger down her spine.

Kate had sent word of a huge battle raging near a small town in Pennsylvania called Gettysburg.

The Battle of Gettysburg was like a saber, slashing into the heart of the nation, North and South. Casualties on both sides had run into the thousands. Montclair was struck by a series of devastating blows as news trickled in. Malcolm had been captured, taken prisoner, as General Lee's forces were thrust back; Leighton was missing, believed killed; Bryce had escaped, but the Confederacy had sustained an agonizing loss in the death of General Stonewall Jackson. A horrifying rumor was later confirmed that he had been fired on by his own men.

Bryce, who had been in the honor guard for the general's funeral in Richmond, arrived at Montclair for a few days' leave. He was depressed, saddened by the fate of his two brothers, and by the loss of his commander. Although he tried nobly to present a great show of bravado and optimism for the others, when he and Garnet were alone in their wing of the house, he confided to her.

"I've applied to join Mosby's scouts."

"What is that?" Garnet asked.

"It's a special unit authorized by General Lee to combat some of the Yankee raiding parties. It's made up of men who know the countryside, the woods, and rivers. It will be undercover operations mostly, scouting out enemy positions, then making surprise attacks and routing them. . . ."

"Sounds dangerous," Garnet murmured.

"Hah!" Bryce made a derisive sound. "All war is dangerous. This kind I understand. Far better than lining men up and mowing them down, row after row. . . ." His voice took on a bitter edge.

Garnet looked at the face on which the firelight shown and realized how haggard it was. Bryce was far different now from the high-spirited, handsome young man who had ridden off to fight a knight's crusade nearly three years ago.

Garnet remembered having met Mosby in Richmond before he headed up his unit, and once Bryce had brought him home to Montclair on their way back from some adventure.

For a "legend" John Mosby's appearance was wholly undistinguished. He was thin and wiry, sharp-featured, with a kind of nervous energy that kept him from being still for ten minutes at a time. But it was his eyes that Garnet had noticed particularly, for they were keen, sparkling, alert as if they missed nothing.

Mosby's Raiders, like their leader himself, John Singleton Mosby, were a unique breed—planters' sons, for the most part, of which Bryce was a perfect example. Bryce had cared little for education, never worked with his hands, loved horses and rode them superbly well, was an excellent hunter and a crack shot. In addition, he possessed the gracious manners of a born gentleman who followed the rigid, unwritten code of the South's elite class. His daring made him a prime volunteer for the Raiders.

Each man kept a horse or two and all were daredevil, reckless riders with a deep-seated loyalty to the Confederate cause, and a wild streak that made them indispensable in the risky assignment they had been given.

Thereafter, Bryce, as a member of the roving band of Mosby's Raiders, often made unexpected, brief visits to Montclair. They never knew when he might suddenly appear, usually at nightfall, with a few of his comrades.

The very qualities that made them superior soldiers also made them wonderful company and welcome guests, and their coming was heralded as occasion for a spontaneous celebration. It was always a boost to the flagging morale and the sad spirits of the small band of women to have these high-spirited young men in the house, and Garnet was relieved to see that Bryce had gradually recovered his old spirit and flair.

It was Dove, rising above her own sorrow, who announced that, in spite of all that had happened, Christmas, 1863, must be observed. For the children's sakes, at least, everyone pitched in to make it a happy occasion.

Bryce had sent word that he would be coming for Christmas and bringing some of his fellow scouts whose homes were too distant for them to spend the holiday with family. So the preparations were especially joyful.

The baking of the cakes and other traditional holiday treats was a problem with sugar so scarce. But they used their few supplies with prodigal abandon. The children entered into the mixing and stirring with great enthusiasm. Afterward, they were allowed to lick the spoons and the bowl when the batter was poured into baking pans.

Garnet set Jonathan and Alair to the task of grinding the sugar cones into powder for the Christmas cake. The two worked with a will, using a little white stone mortar with a stone pestle until they were both flushed with the effort. Then, with Dove and Harmony each holding an end of a muslin cloth, Garnet poured the sugar through until it was pronounced fine and smooth enough for the recipe.

For the first time in a very long while, the kitchen hummed with the sound of happy voices, cheerful activity and was fragrant with warm, delicious aromas. The store of delicacies began to mount in the pie-safe. Montclair had no lack of fruits from the orchards, and, as the women—black and white—and the children sat around the round oak table cracking nuts, seeding raisins, cutting orange peel it would have been hard to imagine that a savage war was being fought not too far distant.

When Bryce and his three companions arrived, they were greeted with happy excitement. The piano was opened and soon the beautiful old Christmas carols rang through the house, filling it with joyous melody. Suddenly Garnet was reminded of Christmases past, when Montclair had been bursting with guests, song, laughter, and the sounds of dancing feet.

Even Sara responded to the gaiety and asked to be

carried down on Christmas Eve to see the lighted Christmas cedar and to watch the children open their homemade gifts—cornhusk dolls for the girls, with pretty wardrobes made for them from Dove's and Harmony's scrapboxes, and a wooden stick horse for Jonathan, carved for him by Joshua, one of the stable grooms. There were pincushions, "housewife's sewing kits" for the men, scarves and socks, knitted from wool grown, carded, and spun from sheep raised at Montclair. Whatever the gift, large or small, the exchange was wonderfully merry.

As they gathered about the dinner table the next day it, too, was reminiscent of pre-War Montclair. Days before, the servants had dug up the silver buried the summer before in fear of a Yankee raid, and had washed and polished it to a glowing sheen. Lovely English bone china dinnerware graced the table, covered with a fine drawn-work linen cloth and set with crystal goblets.

Bryce and his fellow scouts had brought their contributions to the festivities, also, and the feast boasted fresh-brewed coffee, a roasted turkey, a ham, cornbread, sweet potatoes, plum jelly, and a variety of desserts that were "fit for a king," as Bryce later declared.

When at last the children were settled for the night, Bryce confessed that he and his men must leave at daybreak. There was always the chance that a roving Yankee patrol would be ready to ambush, and they wanted to be away before first light.

"But there haven't been any Yankees sighted around here since the earliest part of the War," protested Garnet, hating the thought of another parting. "We're so far back from the road, and besides, Mayfield isn't near anything important."

"Still, dear, it's best we go," Bryce said firmly and Garnet knew there was no use in arguing.

She went to check on Jonathan then. Standing over him as he lay sleeping, she felt an indefinable sadness. Poor little boy, she thought, mother dead; father—who knew where? But at least Malcolm had gone away knowing he had a son, and Rose lived on in their child.

Returning to their bedroom, Garnet observed Bryce from the doorway. He was slumped wearily in the wing chair, his long legs stretched out before him, staring thoughtfully into the fire.

There was something touchingly pensive about his expression, and Garnet longed to comfort him. Tomorrow when he left, Bryce would be riding into certain danger. With a cold, wrenching sensation, Garnet realized that she was the only thing Bryce had left to love. His mother had never made any secret of her preference for Malcolm, and Lee held a special place as her youngest. All Bryce would leave behind, should anything happen to him, was a wife who had never really loved him the way she should have.

Garnet felt a moment of self-accusation and the deep, abiding fear that always lurked in her wayward heart, that she would someday reap what she had sown. The way she had wooed Bryce by wile, won him by false pretenses, treated his love with a careless indifference, longed for another man's love . . . all these were seeds of her own destruction. Every once in awhile Garnet would be frozen with fear of her possible, probable retribution.

Was it possible at this late hour to make up for all she had withheld from Bryce? All that was rightfully his? Garnet was torn between the risk she might be taking and the fear of eternal punishment. What if she were sending Bryce back to War, back to his death without his ever knowing the fulfillment of being loved for himself? Always, in her mind, Malcolm had stood between them.

Now, she saw Bryce for the fine, loving person he was, and she was ashamed. For the first time, Garnet thought about the vows she had taken . . . "to love, honor, cherish, obey." She had taken them without real understanding, commitment or love.

Drawn by something indefinable, Garnet walked over to Bryce and lay her hand on his shoulder. When he looked up into her face, his clear, blue eyes, as lacking in guile as a child's, sent a sharp thrust of guilt through her.

He reached up and took her hand, brought it to his lips, and kissed it, then looked at her again and smiled.

"Come sit down for awhile and watch the fire with me." he invited and drew the hassock alongside his chair.

Garnet sat down, her skirts billowing about her and

held out her hands to the warmth of the blaze. The curtains were drawn against the night and the room had a cozy, intimate atmosphere.

She felt Bryce's hand upon her hair, stroking it, and she lay her head against his knee. Only the crackling and hissing of the fire broke the stillness of the room.

Perhaps Bryce found in the tranquility of the quiet firelit room a realization of the eloquently discussed dream of men gathered around a campfire at night, the warm sweetness of domestic bliss he, himself, had never known. Maybe in this moment he was tasting it for the first time.

For these two who had always had so much to say, the silence was strange but not threatening. Words uttered merely to fill the silence would be hollow and empty. They who had chatted aimlessly, carried on social banter, argued and exchanged heated words, now rested in the quiet. Now that there were so many important things to say, neither could find the words to say them.

From downstairs they heard the striking of the Grandfather clock, reminding them of the hours that they had each flung away unthinkingly in the years past, now measuring out the few hours remaining for them to be together.

As if by mutual accord they turned to look at each other and read within the other's eyes a longing, a need for love they had not recognized before.

Bryce lifted Garnet onto his lap, cradling her head against his shoulder, rocking her gently as he whispered, "Darlin', darlin', I do love you so much. I never knew how much until—"

"I know, I know," she murmured, tilted her head back to answer him.

He stopped whatever else she might have said with his lips—a long, infinitely tender kiss to which she responded as she had not done before.

The room seemed to recede as they clung to each other, murmuring endearments interspersed with kisses—each one deeper, infinitely more demanding, possessively passionate.

Bryce gathered up Garnet and carried her over to the massive bed where their married life had begun four years ago. But that night the love they shared was far different than either of them could have imagined in another lifetime.

It was still dark when Garnet was startled awake by the sound of screaming coming from downstairs—high-pitched, terror-stricken. Without losing a minute, she threw back the quilt and ran out to the hall without slippers or robe. Leaning over the balcony, she saw the front hall swarming with blue uniforms.

She turned and ran back to the bedroom where Bryce was flinging on his clothes.

"Yankees!" she gasped, slamming the door behind her and trying to move the heavy chest in front of it."

"Look, darlin', I'll try to make a break for it out the window!" he told her. "If I don't make it . . ." He grabbed her by her shivering shoulders and spoke low and intensely, "open that mattress! Do what you can!" Then he kissed her, a quick, hard, ardent kiss, and dashed to the window, throwing one leg over the sill and disappearing from sight.

There was no time to do anything. The sound of stomping boots just outside the bedroom door signaled imminent danger. In another minute the door was crashed open, shoving the bureau out of the way, and the room was full of Yankees.

"Out the window!" shouted one.

"He won't get far! We posted men below!" another yelled back and, after taking a hurried look around, taking special note of Garnet who had pressed herself against the wall, they dashed out.

As soon as they had left, she ran to the window and looked out. Her heart sank as she spotted a circle of Yankee soldiers right under the window. Bryce was surrounded, his hands tied behind him. A moment later, she saw the other three men coming out of the house between armed guards.

She watched, stricken, as the Yankees hoisted Bryce and his friends onto horses. Then they all galloped down the drive and out of sight

Garnet stood, rooted to the spot where she had last seen Bryce, until her common sense returned. She must rally her strength. The others would be depending on her—as always.

The whole household was awake by now—the servants, frightened; the children, crying. She dressed hurriedly. Then, composing herself, she descended the stairs to the kitchen to help with the children's breakfasts.

"What will happen to Bryce and the others!" wailed Harmony.

"They'll probably be taken to prison," Garnet answered flatly.

It wasn't until she had gone back upstairs that she remembered Bryce's strange last words. "If I don't make it, open the mattress." What in the world had he meant? But she knew it must be important somehow. At such times, people don't use unnecessary words.

Curious, Garnet looked at the bed, still rumpled from her hasty departure. With both hands, she felt along the mattress under the feather puff. As she searched, she felt a ridge at the very end of the mattress, near the headboard. Taking out her sewing scissors from the basket on her bureau, she ripped at the heavy ticking material, struggling to penetrate it. When at last her scissors punctured the fabric, she tore it open to find a package of papers tied with string.

How clever of Bryce, she thought, wondering when he had secreted them there. Picking up the packet, she saw written on the top:

REPORT TO GENERAL R. E. LEE. EXPEDITE. URGENT!

Hands shaking, knees suddenly weak, Garnet sank down on the bed. Did Bryce really expect her to deliver these papers to General Lee? Her heart began to race. How could she possibly manage that? *Expedite. Urgent!*

However she managed to do it, it had to be done at once!

CHAPTER 4

IT WAS SOON APPARENT why the Yankee patrol had been scouting in the vicinity of Montclair. A sneak attack on Christmas Day had placed the town of Mayfield in Union hands. Mayfield, the "unimportant" place Garnet had imagined would have no possible interest for the Yankees, was a part of a strategic plan to control all the railroad stations on the route to Richmond. With spies in the area, Montclair had been watched for weeks, along with other homes along the road.

This, of course, complicated Garnet's plan to deliver the packet of information addressed to General Lee. It must contain vital information, Garnet thought, or certainly Bryce would never have sent her on such a perilous mission.

She would need a pass to Richmond now that Mayfield was in the hands of the Yankees, Garnet knew. And to obtain one, she would have to go to City Hall, which they had commandeered for headquarters.

Extremely conscious of the papers she had sewn into the shirred satin lining of her bonnet, Garnet walked up the steps of the Mayfield City Hall, inwardly enraged to see the building guarded by blue-uniformed soldiers. As requested, she gave the guard at the door her name and the nature of her errand. Explaining that she must see the officer in charge, he opened the door for her courteously. But Garnet lifted her head high and swept past him, indignant at the thought of engaging in more than the necessary conversation with anyone wearing that hated uniform.

As Garnet entered she saw another soldier seated at a table just inside. At her approach, he looked up, giving her a swift, appraising glance. Something curious flickered in his eyes, and she could not be sure whether it was scorn or admiration. She had dressed very carefully in a green plaid traveling suit, trimmed with narrow velvet cording, and her most becoming bonnet She stated her request once again. This time, the soldier was less polite and brusquely motioned her to a seat where she must wait to be questioned by the commanding officer.

Garnet seated herself warily on the edge of a straight-backed chair and looked around her speculatively. She had never been in the Mayfield City Hall before, and she had certainly never expected to be here under these strange circumstances.

At that moment a tall, smartly uniformed Union officer, bearing a lieutenant's stripes, passed through and glanced in her direction. As he did so, Garnet's hand went to her mouth in a quickly suppressed gasp of surprise. In the look that passed between them, there was a flash of recognition and warning, indicated by the merest drop of his eyelids and swiftly averted head.

Francis Maynard! Garnet's mind telegraphed, wearing a *Yankee* uniform! *Francis* a *spy* for the Confederates? That was the only possible explanation.

Composing her face and studiously erasing any telltale expression, Garnet concentrated on her gloved hands folded tightly in her lap. She was tense with anxiety that she might by some inadvertent gesture give him away. If only she could get Bryce's message to *him,* it would probably reach its destination much faster than by the circuitous route she was still devising, Garnet thought with desperation.

But there was not a chance of the slightest sign of communication. The soldier who had gone to check on the availability of his commander returned, and politely asked her to follow him into an inner office.

It took all Garnet's will power not to look at Francis again as she passed him.

Inside, she waited impatiently to be acknowledged by the gentleman seated at a massive desk. She recognized the insignia of a Colonel. He was quite distinguished, with sandy-gray hair, and a well-trimmed mustache. Lifting her eyes to a spot above his head, she saw, to her horror, the United States flag. She had not seen one flying hereabouts for nearly three years. Now, the colonel looked up, a brief, indifferent glance, before bending his head once again over the papers on his desk.

"What is the purpose of your trip to Richmond?" The question came in a sharp staccato.

"To see relatives, one who has been ill," she replied, her voice sounding whispery to her ears. She cleared her throat, hoping to make her next answer firmer.

The Colonel looked up again, gave her a penetrating stare.

"How long do you intend to remain in Richmond?"

"Only a few days. Long enough to satisfy myself that my relative is recovering."

"With whom will you be staying?"

"My cousin, Mrs. Nell Perry."

"You are carrying no contraband?"

Garnet's throat constricted; her heart thundered. What should she say now? She was not quite sure what constituted contraband, but she felt sure Bryce's notes would be considered hostile to the enemy.

Noting her hesitance, the Colonel glowered at her under his bushy eyebrows.

If they suspected her of lying, the Colonel might order her searched. Reports of such things were numerous. The Yankees were on the alert for any rebellious activities among civilians, she knew. She drew a long shaky breath, but before she could answer, a knock came at the door.

"Come in!" barked the Colonel, and Francis Maynard entered.

Salutes were exchanged, then he placed a sheaf of papers before the Colonel. "These require your signature at once, sir."

The Colonel accepted them and began riffling through

them. Then, as if remembering Garnet's presence, quickly took an ink stamp, pounded a slip of paper authoritatively, and handed it to her.

"Madam, your pass."

Weak with relief, and not daring to meet Francis's eyes again, she quickly took the paper. Holding herself stiffly erect, she left the room and found her way out of the building. Yet she could not truly relax for the danger had not passed—not until she was safely behind Confederate lines once more.

Settled on the train bound for Richmond at last, Garnet thought about Francis Maynard, whom she had rejected as a beau because he had no spirit, no daring! Now he was playing a dangerous game, indeed. The penalty for losing—a firing squad! How wrong she had been about him—about so many things.

There was no one to meet Garnet at the station. Cousin Nell's carriage and horses had long since been contributed to the war effort. Since there were also no hacks for hire, she picked up her valise and, with Bessie carrying the other bundles, Garnet started out on foot in the direction of Franklin Street.

She was acutely and distressingly aware that Richmond had changed drastically since her last visit. The sidewalks were crowded with people, some of a type she had never before seen in the charming town she had once known.

Suddenly their progress was halted and Garnet felt her heart wrung with sadness as she heard the familiar sound of the funeral dirge played by a military band coming down the street. She edged to the curb and watched as the sorrowful pageant passed—the coffin, draped with black crepe and crowned with cap, sword, gloves; the riderless horse following, with empty boots fixed in the stirrups of an army saddle; the honor guard marching behind with arms reversed and folded banners.

This, then, was how some of the young men she had flirted with and kissed goodbye came home, Garnet thought, her throat raw with anguish. Here at last the War was seen in all its stark reality, and no one watching the grim procession could miss its fatal message.

At Cousin Nell's she was greeted with loving cries of welcome. "Oh, my dear, I'm just now on my way to hospital duty. All Richmond ladies are needed to nurse the wounded." Her eyes moistened and she gave her head a sorrowful shake. "So many, so young. But I shall be home this evening." She hugged Garnet warmly. "I am so very happy to see you, child. How you will brighten the place. Some young people are coming tonight and your cousin Jessie is here from Savannah. Perhaps you won't mind sharing your room with her. It's the one you and Bryce had. And how is the dear boy? Oh, dear, I do believe I'm late!" and without waiting for a reply, she bustled off.

When she was last safe behind the closed bedroom door upstairs, Garnet carefully ripped out the tiny stitches along the inner edge of her bonnet. When the slit was wide enough, she drew out the small flattened sheets of paper, trying not to tear them. Glancing at the jumbled series of words and figures written hastily with the stub of a pencil, she assumed they were some kind of code, probably gleaned in the heat of an intelligence-seeking mission.

Smoothing them out, she then slipped them into an envelope. As soon as possible she must get them to the President's office. Surely someone there would know how to get them to General Lee. Pray God, it was not too late!

Suddenly feeling the exhaustion of her recent ordeal, Garnet stretched out across the bed, reliving her part of Bryce's dangerous assignment. It seemed abundantly clear that she had been divinely protected. Certainly it had not been by chance that she had been interrupted at the precise moment the Colonel was interrogating her about contraband. That she had received a pass so quickly, so easily was surely a miracle. She knew of others who had waited for weeks for such clearance.

She had heard of other incidents where women had been searched. The Yankees knew there were too many information leaks, too many maneuvers precipitated, too many battles lost due to skillful, surreptitious spying. It was a miracle she had not been even requested to drop her hoop from under her starched petticoats, as had been reported by a Mayfield lady only recently. It seems there had been a document discovered, sewed into the circling bands, on its way to the Confederate capitol.

Garnet closed her eyes and whispered a prayer of gratitude. Angels must have gone before her to make a way, just as as she had read recently in Scripture: If ye have faith—even faith as small as a grain of mustard seed, nothing shall be impossible. She had found it in Matthew 17:20. That passage Garnet had committed to memory, convinced that her own faith was very small, but trusting His promise: If thou canst believe . . . all things are possible. Even the *impossible!* Her eyes grew heavy and she felt herself drifting into an exhausted sleep. As she did so, she murmured, "Lord, I believe. Help Thou mine unbelief."

That evening it was like old times in Cousin Nellie's parlor, although there were many new faces and everyone seemed so much younger. Among the guests were quite a few refugees, people who had fled Yankee occupation of their homes. But tonight, discussion of the War was curiously absent. It seemed that all wanted to forget, for at least a few fleeting hours, the reality of the Confederate plight.

In spite of her secret anxiety, Garnet soon was caught up in the spirit of gaiety and fun. There was much merriment as they played a game of "Similes" and afterward, gathered around the piano for a songfest.

Earlier in the evening, Garnet had been introduced to some newcomers—the lovely Marylander, Constance Cary, and her escort, Burton Harrison, the young secretary to President Jefferson. As Garnet glanced across the piano, she saw him standing there, and an idea flashed through her mind. Who better than *he* to deliver her packet? But how could she pass it to him without being obvious?

Jessie had whispered that he was engaged to Constance and wasn't likely to leave her side all evening. Furthermore, Garnet wasn't eager to chance any malicious rumors by employing her old flirtatious wiles to take him aside.

The solution came shortly, for, as some of the guests

were leaving, Cousin Nell tucked her arm through Garnet's and whispered, "We have been invited to Mrs. Davis's reception tomorrow!" She dimpled delightedly. "It is to be a musicale for the benefit of the hospital. Burton especially asked that you be included."

A perfect opportunity! Garnet decided. Surely at a large reception, with people milling about, there would be a chance to seek out Burton Harrison and give him the papers.

There were light snow flurries the next afternoon as they set out for the Presidential mansion. The house purchased for the First Family of the Confederacy was elegant with spacious rooms, high ceilings, and a lovely curving stairway leading from the front hall to the upper stories.

As Garnet, Cousin Nell, Jessie and her escort, Captain Alec Hunter, a physician assigned to the Wayside Hospital, entered the foyer, Garnet saw Burton Harrison standing beside Mrs. Davis in the receiving line.

"I don't see the President," said Cousin Nell in a low tone. "He has been quite unwell of late. Migraine. Suffers dreadfully for days, they say. Then some sort of neuralgia, as well."

If circumstances had been different, perhaps, Garnet would have been disappointed not to see President Davis himself. She had often seen him riding, sometimes alone, sometimes with an aide, but had never been formally presented to him. Like all Southern women, Jefferson Davis epitomized for Garnet the Southern gentleman— tall, aristocratic features, impeccable manners, gracious demeanor. But today Garnet's eyes were focused on his secretary, Burton Harrison.

They stood in the slow-moving line of guests and when at last they reached Mr. Harrison, he greeted Garnet cordially, mentioning a humorous incident at the party the night before and expressing hope that she planned to remain for the musical program to follow.

"Oh, yes, indeed!" Garnet replied, giving him her most winning smile and thereby incurring the disapproving stare of Cousin Nell. "Shall we see you later?"

"Perhaps you could save me a seat beside you?" he suggested.

"With pleasure!" she responded.

In the adjoining room, chairs had been placed in a semicircle in front of the elevated platform on which a piano, a harp and chairs for two violinists were arranged.

Garnet, who had secreted, the small packet in her muff, sent up a silent prayer that somehow, during the concert, she could easily hand it to Burton with a whispered explanation.

After they had partaken of the refreshments set out for the guests, Garnet and Cousin Nell found seats, and Garnet casually placed her cloak and muff on the one next to her to keep unoccupied until Burton Harrison could extricate himself from his receiving line duties.

Garnet smiled apologetically to several persons seeking a seat, murmuring sweetly that it was taken.

After several such incidents, Cousin Nell asked, "Who are you saving it for? Jessie and her beau have already found seats."

"Burton Harrison." Garnet whispered back, and Cousin Nell raised an eyebrow.

Garnet mentally shrugged. She could not risk explaining. If Cousin Nell took the wrong implication, it could not be helped. Besides, her reputation as a flirt was well-established and, even now, she was probably being discussed behind certain ladies' fans as running true to form—"And her husband away in the War, too!"

In the end it all worked out perfectly. Just as the musicians took their places, Burton Harrison slipped into the chair beside Garnet. The program began and there was no chance to speak to him until the intermission. Then Garnet turned to him quickly. Putting her hand over her mouth so that no one else could possibly hear, she leaned close and whispered her message.

"I realize I am taking advantage of our slight acquaintance, Mr. Harrison, but I have in my possession a packet of papers designated for the President's or General Lee's immediate attention. May I ask you to deliver them?"

Burton's eyes widened and a look of incredulity passed over his face. But there was no time for further enlightenment. He gave a quick nod.

Garnet put her hand inside her muff, felt the edges of the small bundle, and grasped it, drawing it out of his hiding place. Then, under the cover of their printed programs held at an angle she passed the packet to Burton, who skillfully inserted it into an inside pocket of his jacket.

While the musicians were tuning their instruments, he excused himself and quietly left the room. Garnet felt the release of tension that, without realizing it, had kept her in a viselike grip for days. She gave a deep sigh. Cousin Nell shot her a sharp look and, completely misinterpreting the entire episode, bent over and hissed into Garnet's ear, "The beautiful Miss Cary must have just arrived! Burton has made a hasty retreat."

Garnet only smiled. Let Cousin Nell think what she liked. It was over at last! She had successfully fulfilled the trust Bryce had given her.

Part IV

MONTCLAIR

1864-1865

*Faith . . . the substance of things hoped for, the evidence
of things not seen.*

Hebrews 11:1

CHAPTER 1

IT TURNED BITTERLY COLD in mid-January and, for the next two months, the weather alternated from freezing rain to snow to sleet. Throughout the South, the common suffering endured seemed to strengthen an indomitable spirit. The belief that their Cause was noble and no sacrifice in vain did not diminish a heartfelt longing for peace. But that winter, peace was still far away.

At Montclair, the outer storms mirrored the turmoil of mind and emotions of the three young women. Garnet, on whom the burden rested most heavily, tried to meet each day with courage and her new-found faith.

Not a single word had come from Bryce since his capture. Rumors that Mosby men had arranged a daring raid on a prison camp, and that the captives had been hiding in the woods, waging guerrilla warfare, were rampant. But Garnet knew nothing.

In her heart she was determined when Bryce came home—*if he came home*—it would be to a different kind of wife. Meanwhile, Montclair waited in a kind of wary suspense for the return of the Montrose men.

It was, however, an immediate crisis that took their minds off the constant, insidious anxiety that permeated every moment of every day.

One blustery March day as they gathered for supper.

Garnet noticed that all the children looked unusually flushed. Both Alair and Jonathan were cross, and Alair gave the little boy a shove as they took their places at the table. He pushed her back, and a squabble ensued.

Dove quickly stepped between them, took a hand in each of her own, and began their evening prayer: "Bless, we beseech Thee, those from whom we are now separated. Grant that they may be kept from all harm, and restore them to us in Thine own good time. Amen."

Momentary quiet prevailed as Tilda came in with a tureen of stew, and Garnet began to fill the plates Harmony passed to her. But then little Dru started fussing, rubbed her eyes, pushed away her food, then climbed up on Dove's lap, sucking her thumb and lying limply against Dove's shoulder during the rest of the meal.

"What's the matter with you two?" Garnet asked Alair finally, when another little tussle of wills erupted.

Alair gave her golden head a stubborn little toss and lifted her chin. Jonathan turned his large dark eyes upon her accusingly, and Garnet noticed they were glazed and heavy-lidded.

Tilda, who was serving biscuits and passing behind Jonathan, placed her hand on his forehead. "Why, dis here chile is burnin' up wid de fever, Miz Garnet!"

"Oh, dear!" sighed Harmony. "If Jonathan's coming down with something, the others are sure to get it, too. Come over here, Alair, baby, this minute. Come away from Jonathan. He's got something that's catchin'."

Garnet had to bite her tongue not to snap at Harmony. As though keeping Alair at the opposite end of the table would protect her if Jonathan did, indeed, have something contagious. After all, they played together constantly, lived in the same house!

Garnet rose from her place and went over to Jonathan. Bending down beside his chair, she asked anxiously, "You feel bad, honey?"

He nodded, his little head drooped and he leaned against Garnet's shoulder heavily.

"Tilda, I think we best get this boy to bed right away." Garnet said, lifting him and passing him into Tilda's waiting arms. "I better go get the Remedy Book and see what we can find to help us."

Dove followed with Druscilla as Garnet went into the library and looked for the book. With Dove peering over her shoulder, she skimmed the contents until she came to "Children's Fevers." They both read silently, then Garnet raised her head and met Dove's worried gaze.

"The first and most important thing, I guess, is to get their fevers down. It could be any of a number of things—scarlet fever, or . . . ," and they both looked panic-stricken, "or worse, diphtheria or typhoid."

A forty-eight hour nightmare followed. All three children were very sick. Headaches, chills, then high fevers had them tossing restlessly, and mumbling deliriously.

So that the children could receive constant nursing care, they were placed in the same room. Only Harmony was not any real help, Garnet fretted, hovering over Alair most of the time, getting in the way of the others as they changed damp nightgowns and bedclothes, or tried to administer remedies. Harmony cried when Dove suggested cutting off some of Alair's curls, which were becoming tangled from her delirious movement and her refusal to be touched with brush or comb.

The nursing was constant as were the work and chores associated with three children so desperately ill. All the bed linens and garments had to be changed daily, then boiled and hung out to dry. In the uncertain March weather, this meant sheets were spread before every fireplace, then often had to be ironed dry to be used again.

Each child had to be bathed three times daily, their dry, burning skin soothed with oil, poultices of hot towels soaked in soda water, mixed with a teaspoonful of dry mustard, and wrapped in flannel to relieve some of the pain. While compresses of tepid water were regularly renewed to alleviate the raging headaches.

The three women, Garnet, Tilda, and Dove, were running up and down the stairs dozens of times a day, while Linny and Carrie took over the laundry and cooking. The three little patients could eat nothing due to the soreness of their throats and their upset stomachs, but Sara, complaining as ever, required her meals strictly on time and prepared delicately as always.

Three dreadful weeks of anxiety crawled by before the three children showed any signs of recovery. By then their aunts and mothers were ready to fall into their own beds from exhaustion and worry.

Garnet found continuous employment for the very first Scripture verse she had ever learned. Some days it was all she had time to pray, during those weeks: "I can do all things through Christ which strengtheneth me."

Little by little each child began to come out of the long period of illness, sat up in bed, and, finding the other children similarly confined, thought it something of a lark. To be read to and brought up trays of fresh soft-boiled eggs and dainty custards began to be fun, after all the weeks of boiled tea and broth.

To Harmony's dismay Alair's hair began to fall out in huge clumps. The result was an angelic halo of close-cropped pale gold curls that gave her a cherubic appearance far different from the little girl's true mischievous personality.

Garnet could only thank God for His profound mercy in sparing all three children the dangerous complications that were possible with such a serious illness. She found she cherished even more the wonderful treasure she had been given in Malcolm's little son.

The dark days and dread under which the whole household had functioned suddenly lifted, and, to their surprise, they discovered that while they had all been preoccupied with the children, spring had come to Montclair in all its glory.

CHAPTER 2

THE YEAR THE SEASON SEEMED especially beautiful to Garnet. The blooming flowers, the sunny days, the singing of the birds like some lovely symphony seemed to say that the War had been just a dreadful dream and not real at all. And yet, the cold of winter lingered in her heart.

When she allowed herself to think about it, her faith faltered. The loneliness, the weariness, the waiting for word that Bryce or Malcolm might have somehow escaped or been exchanged wore heavily. Although now the Yankees had stopped exchanging prisoners, knowing how the South needed all able-bodied men to shore up their depleted forces.

Because of Montclair's isolated location, communication from the outside world had virtually stopped. Although they had heard of the terrible Bread Riots in Richmond, when hungry desperate women with starving children had stormed the capital and broken into the storage depots, those at Montclair had not felt the acute plight of the poor city-dwellers.

From occasional letters Garnet knew Cousin Nell saw first-hand the bitter hardships the War had brought to Richmond, the drastic way the city had been transformed from the quiet charming place it had been.

Sadly "war profiteers" abounded. Gunmakers, contractors, wholesalers plied their trade aggressively and grew wealthy. Corruption, black marketing, greed and indifference to the suffering to others caused by the very goods they manufactured and created and hoarded was rife.

If there were anything to worry about, it was whether or not there would be sufficient field hands to harvest the crops come fall. Mr. Montrose had come and taken nearly eighty of his ablest workers to work on the fortifications at the southern harbors where it was feared a Yankee attack might be forthcoming. He promised they would be back in time as wagon-load after wagon-load left.

Neither he nor anyone else discussed what was often a haunting horror in the backs of the minds of most Southerners.

Rumors of a possible slave uprising had run the gamut among the white people when the Emancipation Proclamation became effective in January, two years previous. Hatred of Lincoln was at a fever pitch throughout the South, and tales of Yankees infiltrating and stirring up such trouble ran rampant. However, at Montclair and at Cameron Hall as well, the slaves still seemed unaware of what had taken place. At least on the surface, everything was just as before, with the servants going about their tasks and chores quietly and as usual. If there were whisperings or news circulating of imminent liberation for their people, it was only in the privacy of their own quarters.

Certainly Garnet had no reason to doubt the loyalty of the house servants who had risen to the occasions of every new challenge with surprising ease and had shown themselves unexpectedly adaptable to the added responsibilities. Tilda had been particularly dependable, willing and able to help Garnet in everything. Linny had full charge of the three children, Carrie had become Sara's maid-nurse-companion, Bessie, formerly Garnet's personal maid, had become a fair cook.

There was so much to be done every day—the gardening, canning, preserving and drying of food for next winter—that there was no time to dwell long on the shadow of uncertainty about the outcome of the War. But since Gettysburg, discouragement and disillusionment hung over the entire South like smoke over a battlefield.

It was the children who made life at Montclair bearable. They were allowed almost total freedom because the adults were so busy and preoccupied. They spent most of the day running barefoot, to save shoe leather now too scarce to waste. Because of the clothing shortages, they wore as little as the black children used to wear, growing tanned and healthy under the summer sun. It was a joy to watch them play together under the shade of the leafy trees near the house.

One day Garnet had just stepped out on to the veranda for a breath of fresh air, seeking a brief respite from the heat of the kitchen where they had been boiling a mixture of berries for jam.

As she stood there watching the children at play, Garnet saw one of the menservants from Cameron Hall coming up the driveway on horseback, and a cold, clutching sensation gripped her. No one ever came from Cameron Hall these days; no one could be spared. Her mother's servants were as busy as those at Montclair. As the man came closer she saw it was Nemo, a younger servant who had helped old Porter in the care of Garnet's father since his stroke.

He dismounted and, wide-brimmed straw hat in hand, advanced toward the porch. It was then that Garnet saw his face contorted in grief and tears running down his cheeks.

Her heart lodged in her throat, Garnet moved to the top of the porch steps and asked through numb lips, "Is it my father, Nemo?" The man bowed his head, nodding, "Yes, ma'm, Miz Garnet. I's sorry to be the one to tell yo'."

Garnet went to Cameron Hall at once. Kate held her as Garnet wept in her mother's arms, and tried to comfort her saying, "It's over for him, darling," Kate said softly. "He doesn't have to see any more of the tragic things that are happening to the South he loved, the people he cared for so deeply, the way of life he knew. We can't feel sad about that, Garnet."

116

Two days later, sitting beside her mother, pale, tearless, composed, Garnet looked out the open French doors through which she could hear faint birdsong, smell the fragrance of garden flowers on the soft summer breeze billowing the curtains inward. How could birds still sing, lilacs nod their lavender plumes to the gentle wind, when part of her world had ended?

The minister's voice was reading with the infinite sadness of one who had often, and many times recently, read these same words: "Blessed are they that die in the Lord . . ."

Had her father died in the Lord? Garnet wondered. Had he come to accept Jesus as His Savior before he was struck down with that lightening blow of paralytic stroke? She knew something had happened to change his former agnostic attitude, but when or how it had happened she could not be sure. She remembered him saying sometimes to her mother.

"I wish I could believe as whole-heartedly as you do, my dear Kate! That is not to say I don't believe, I just wish I could be *convinced*. . . ."

Had he been convinced? He looked so wonderfully at peace when she had looked down into that beloved face yesterday. Garnet felt the constriction in her throat, the need to cry as stinging tears sprang into her eyes. She felt her mother's soft hand cover hers in gentle pressure, heard the minister's voice again, . . . "And God will wipe away every tear from their eyes; and there shall be no more death, nor sorrow, nor crying: and there shall be no more pain, for the former things have passed away."

Yes, the former things had passed away. That much was true. But what of the rest? Had her father found that those blessed promises are fulfilled?

Garnet fervently hoped so, prayed so.

CHAPTER 3

NOW GARNET KNEW that there would be no son for Bryce, no strong, young boy to ride his father's land, to learn to hunt in his woods or fish in its streams, to grow up and inherit Montclair.

The hope she had wanted to offer Bryce, a reason to go on fighting, to come home to, all vanished and Garnet felt a sense of purposelessness and futility.

It became harder and harder for her to drag herself through each day's duties. She felt helpless and fearful much of the time and yet something stubborn within her refused to give in to her circumstances. Ironically, she thought, since Abraham Lincoln had issued the Emancipation Proclamation, the slaves were free but she wasn't. She was tied to a house that wasn't hers, the responsibility of three small children, an invalid. Dove and Harmony depended on her, too.

But with the coming of summer, Garnet rallied. The gardens and orchards at Montclair produced an abundance that year and all of them spent much of every day outside—picking berries, gathering fruit. The children grew rosy and healthy playing in the fresh air and sunshine, and some days Garnet almost felt happy.

Summer slid away and one dry, warm September day Garnet left the house and walked up along the hillside above the meadows. From there she could look down and see the ribbon of the river in the distance, the wooded area now here and there slashed with the crimson of a maple or red-berry tree against the dark green pines.

At the crest of the hill, she turned and sank down on the grass. From where she sat she could see Montclair and the blackened wing with its windows boarded up where the fire had been—the fire that had changed so much for so many.

For her, the change had been as sudden as the flames that had swept through that part of the house. For years she had dreamed of being Mistress of Montclair. Now she was, and with that role had come all the unexpected burdens and responsibilities unknown in that childhood dream!

A kind of numbed desolateness seized her and she felt a desperate hunger to bring back her yesterdays. She saw them now as she saw Montclair, from a distance, with none of the inevitable flaws, and knew they were just as much a dream as her childish ones.

The idealistic view she had held of her father as invincible, of Malcolm as perfection itself, of her desires as attainable—she now saw as unrealistic fantasy.

She thought of that passage she had recently read in Rose's Bible and now began to understand. "When I was a child, I spake as a child, I understood as a child, I thought as a child." Now it was time "to put away childish things." But it was hard. Garnet closed her eyes and a parade of all the lovely things that had been part of her youth passed before her . . . the gentle pattern of days at home, the sound of laughter and soft voices, the sense of comforting security, the low hum of singing from the quarters in summer twilight. . . .

The happiness she had taken so carelessly, never realizing it could not last.

Gone, all gone. . . .

Garnet turned and lay, face down, on the grass. Grabbing handfuls of it, she buried head in the meadow fragrance. The sun on her back cast a shadow as she spread out her arms on either side. *Like a cross*, she thought whimsically.

That's the way she felt sometimes, stretched to the utmost, broken. She heard that word so much. Especially lately. Dove was "broken-hearted." And so was Sara, over Leighton's death and Malcolm's imprisonment.

Brokenness? What do they mean by brokenness. Whenever Garnet had heard that topic preached, she had dismissed it just like any other thing she did not understand. But she had heard the word so much lately. This one or that one was "broken"—by bereavement, by sorrow, by losses of all sorts. Even her mother had used the word, saying that her father was "broken in spirit."

But there was another meaning, deeper and more subtle, Garnet was beginning to believe. It was a feeling she was experiencing more and more. That of being spent, devoid of her own strength, relying more and more on God. Almost without her knowing it, it had happened. The weariness, the heartache and, just when she thought she could not bear one more thing, something else always happened.

Yet somehow she had managed to go on, taking care of the children, Sara and the servants. But as though she had some kind of invisible support. They all kept taking from her, drawing their courage, strength and ability to keep going from her, and still she was able to give it. It was as though their needing supplied her giving.

It was strange. Again and again she turned to the mystery of it. She had heard once that Jesus had become "broken bread and poured out wine" for the salvation of men to nourish and sustain them.

In a way He was squeezing her by circumstances, by the burden of helpless adults and little children, by privation and loss—squeezing her like a grape into wine. Before all this had happened, before the War, before Rose's death and Leighton's and all they had to contend with here at Montclair, she had not been "ripe" to be squeezed. She had resisted, railed against her lot, been angry with God, hard. Anything that had come from her then would have been bitter, not fit to nourish or sustain anyone.

But gradually, God had done something in her. She was not even sure what it was, but she had slowly and gradually softened. She had stopped fighting the way things were. She had tried to make the best of what came along. She had tried . . . to love! Loving the children wasn't hard, especially Jonathan, and baby Dru. Alair was a bit difficult sometimes and Harmony impossible . . . unless you laughed at her ineptness. Dove was a darling and not a problem. The servants were, after all, her responsibility, and like children, more easily led by love than harshness. Whatever had happened, God was using her, in spite of herself, to be the kind of "bread and wine" that would benefit others.

Garnet knew she had not completely changed. But she knew she was changing for the better. As the outer things of her life had been stripped away, she had discovered a tiny spark within herself that she was fanning into flame. As her self-interest diminished, her compassion, tolerance and understanding for others grew.

She no longer had any illusions about herself. She saw herself for what she had been, what she still was. The word "brokenness" again came to mind—this time in a different context.

The more she had read God's Word, the more convicted Garnet had become. The commandments she had learned by rote as a child she now realized she had broken, all of them. Or nearly all.

But as she slowly got to her feet that day and started back to the house, Garnet said with David in his Psalm:

Thou delightest not in burnt offerings. . . .
The sacrifices of God are a *broken* spirit
A broken and contrite heart,
O God, you will not despise.

CHAPTER 4

December 1864

IT WAS JUST BEFORE MIDDAY the second week in December. The weather all month had been unusually mild. The rains had ceased and, although the mornings were frosty, by noon each day the sun was bright and warm. The children, released from the confinement of the house during the dreary, gray days of November, were playing happily outside.

In the pantry Garnet was helping Tilda store freshly baked pies in the pie-safe when they both heard something, stopped suddenly and stood listening. Then their eyes met, Tilda's widening and Garnet's narrowing, as simultaneously the same thought struck each woman.

"Oh, Lawdee, Miss Garnet—" whispered Tilda in a voice that held the terror that gripped Garnet. The dread word neither of them could utter rose in both throats.

Montclair's remote location, so far from the road, had been both a blessing and a problem. They had felt protected from some of the earlier Yankee foraging raids suffered by friends on neighboring plantations. But their isolation had also often prevented their getting news or word of trouble in the area. For weeks, no rumor had reached them of Yankee activity in the area.

Even as these thoughts raced through Garnet's mind, she heard Linny's high-pitched scream, "Yankees! Yankees!" mingled with the terrified cries of the children. Almost on top of that, the thundering sound of horses hooves grew loud and, as Garnet and Tilda looked out of the windows, they saw the blue-coated men on horseback literally surrounding the house.

Garnet went rigid as the noise and clash of arms rose to a frightening crescendo. Then her brain reacted, activating her muscles, and she rushed out toward the front of the house.

There she found Linny squatting just inside the front door, with baby Druscilla clinging to her. Dove and Harmony were huddled at the foot of the staircase with the two other children, their faces blanched with fear. From the long windows across the front of the house, they could see the driveway, and the sight sent waves of horrified helplessness over them.

The crescent in front of the house was a sea of blue uniforms—at least thirty or more galloping down the road and into the yard, running their horses over garden, bush, shrubs and lawn. They came like a rushing wind, with loud shouts, blood-chilling yells, rifles lifted, bayonets glinting in the sun. Each new group arrived in the same way, their horses careening, sliding as their riders yanked their reins, sending them into dust-raising spins, their slipping hooves spitting gravel. Some reared, adding their whinnying to the men's strident cheers, shattering the quiet of the afternoon with the piercing noise.

Yankees! The word screamed in Garnet's mind, splintering her courage. Yankees here at Montclair. Her knees wobbled and she swayed, putting out her hand to steady herself on the stair post.

A series of bangs of the brass knocker crashing against the front door made delay dangerous. Garnet set Jonathan on his feet, and, hoping the sight of this appealing little boy might soften the hearts of whomever was so unfeelingly demanding entrance, she took his hand, saying to him in a quick, clear voice, "Now, Jonathan, you come with me. They're nothing but some mean old Yankees, and we're not to be afraid, hear? Your Papa and Uncle Bryce could lick 'em all single-handed, but they're not here right now to protect us. So you've got to be the man of the house, and we're just going out there and stare 'em in the eye.''

Jonathan nodded solemnly.

"Well, come on then," she said, tugging him along by the hand, Garnet hurried out to the hall and unlocked the door and opened it.

A Union soldier, a noncommissioned officer, stood there. He had a broad, weatherbeaten face and looked hardened, battle-worn. He gave Garnet a swift, appraising look and no greeting.

"We have come for horses and provisions," he said gruffly. "But we also have orders to search the premises. We've been told this house has harbored *rebels*."

"There is no one here but defenseless women and children and an invalid, sir. I would hope your men would have the decency not to disturb her further, for her health is very delicate and has probably already suffered great distress at your arrival." Garnet was astonished at how steady her voice was, for her heart was slamming so hard she thought she might faint from its pounding.

"Well, ma'm, as I said, we came for horses and provisions only, not to frighten women and children. So, we'll just be about our business, which should be profitable—" he added with a slight sneer. "We've heard Montclair keeps a full stable of fine-blooded horses and well-stocked storehouses."

Garnet felt indignation arise in her. What right had these invaders to come on private property and take whatever they wanted? She lifted her chin and took a few steps forward.

"You are mistaken. Most of our horses went with *our* men into battle. What is left are mainly farm animals, work horses that are needed to work the land and harvest our crops so that we will not be without food."

Again the man's mouth slid sideways, and he gave a scornful, mirthless laugh.

"It's a matter of indifference to us, ma'am, whether you rebels go hungry or starve. We need *work* horses as well as riding horses, to pull our supply wagons. We'll take whatever we need. But before we do, we have orders to enter this dwelling and search it.''

"On whose authority?" Garnet countered, her hand tightening on Jonathan's. "I told you there was no one here but women and children.''

"Ma'am, I mean you no personal harm. Just stand aside so my men can enter and search." He turned and waved a squad of five soldiers forward. Five more followed and five after that. They pushed past Garnet and within minutes the house seemed to be swarming with blue-clad soldiers.

"Where do you keep your arms?" the sergeant shouted above the rattle of clanking sabers and spurs as some of the soldiers started upstairs.

"Arms? We have no arms! I told you we are only defenseless women and children here." Garnet started toward the staircase in a futile attempt to stop the never-ending tide of blue coats. "My mother-in-law is a helpless invalid confined to her bed! I beg you, do not allow your men to frighten her by intruding upon her!" Garnet pleaded. Frantically she looked up to the balcony and saw Dove with Dru in her arms run down the hallway toward Sara's suite. Thank God! Garnet thought. Maybe Dove could keep them from entering Sara's room, terrifying her.

The sergeant was paying no attention. He stood at the archway leading into the parlor and was directing his men in their search. Garnet saw them lift the lid of the grand piano, poking down through the strings ruthlessly with rifle butts. She heard the cacophony of strings being broken, the crack of fine wood splintering. They were everywhere, knocking against the delicate end tables, overturning the fragile lyre-backed chairs, yanking open drawers of the French chests flanking the fireplace.

A teakwood chest in the hall was flung open, its contents of linens, tea napkins and embroidered cloths tossed out carelessly onto the floor, then trampled underfoot as the muddy boots of the men moved on into the dining room.

Garnet followed them in a kind of horrified trance. She saw one soldier try to open the glass-fronted china cabinet and, when it would not open, he took his rifle butt and broke the glass. She spun around and, facing the sergeant who stood in the middle of the hall, his hands on his hips, she implored with flaming eyes.

"Do your men have to do that? How would you like your home to be so invaded, your furniture broken and destroyed?"

"We are only doing our duty, ma'am, following orders," he replied without a change of his stony expression. "We were informed there were weapons stored in this house, and possibly fugitives from the United States Government in rebellion." Then he stretched out his huge hand, palm up and demanded harshly. "If you'll give me the keys to any other locked cupboards, chests, trunks or closets in which such might be hidden, then my men wouldn't have to use force."

Garnet looked at the shattered priceless china cups, the Sevres and Spode Sara had purchased on her European honeymoon, all heirlooms. She felt sick. How could these men do this? They weren't human, she thought with disgust. She gave a scathing look at the sergeant and said through clenched teeth "I'll get what keys I have. But from the sound of smashing upstairs, I'm sure I'm too late."

Still holding Jonathan's clammy little hand, she pulled him with her as she walked into the library to Mr. Montrose's desk where a ring of household keys was kept. There she saw more wanton damage. All his fine books had been swept off the shelves, scattered on the floor, kicked aside as the men continued their pointless search.

The sergeant was right behind her and she asked in a voice that shook with fury. "Is this really necessary?" she flung out her arm in a despairing gesture.

Ignoring her question, he said, tight-lipped. "Your keys, ma'am."

Garnet went over to her father-in-law's massive mahogany desk and drew the keys from the pigeon-hole behind its small door. The sergeant was practically stepping on her skirt as she turned to hand them to him. He grabbed them out of her hand, raking the edges along the soft skin of her palm.

Unable to endure what was happening in there, Garnet

left just as some of the soldiers had shouldered open the locked door into Mr. Montrose's plantation office off the library. As she went into the hall, she could hear more breakage and stomping behind her.

At the foot of the staircase, Garnet was halted by a high-pierced wail from the kitchen area. She whirled around and, dragging Jonathan behind her, ran in that direction. Before she could reach the entryway, she heard the crash of clattering dishes. When she reached the door of the pantry, she saw Carrie cowering against the wall while a hulking soldier shook her by the shoulders so vigorously the girl's head struck the wall.

"Where's the liquor? Speak up, you little— " He called her a terrible name and shouted, "Where does your master keep his spirits?"

"Leave her alone!" gasped Garnet, bending over Carrie.

Suddenly a fellow soldier called out, "Here it is!"

Garnet heard the shattering sound of glass and the splintering of wood, and knew they had broken open the inlaid and beveled glass cabinet in which Mr. Montrose kept his table wines.

At the same time Carrie came running over, sobbing. "Gawd hep us, Miz Garnet! Dey is takin ebrything! Robbin' us ob all de food. I done tole 'em what little we had was mostly fo' de chillun."

"Never mind, Carrie. You take Jonathan. I'll try to stop them," Garnet said, her voice choked with anger. Her blood was pounding in her head, her breath shallow. She picked up her skirts and ran back into the kitchen. There she met a sight that defied description.

Soldiers were flinging sacks of potatoes, onions and yams over their shoulders and disappearing with them out the back door and through the breezeway, tossing them across the saddles of their horses they had tethered to the posts. Then back they rushed, heaving sacks of corn meal and flour in the same way.

Another group of soldiers was piling pots and pans into an empty flour sack from which they had emptied its former contents onto the floor. The sight of all this waste overwhelmed Garnet, knowing as she did the diminished state of their supplies. Now, their larder would surely be bare.

Through the other door, she saw two soldiers emptying out the drawers of the Sheraton sideboard in the dining room, throwing the ornate Montrose silverware helter-skelter into pillowcases they must have stripped from the beds upstairs. Garnet felt suddenly so weak she had to cling to the door frame. Gathering every ounce of strength, she tried to make herself heard over the noise.

"Haven't you done enough damage?"

The sergeant simply glowered at her and snarled, "We have our orders. We're just doing our duty."

"Is it the duty of Union soldiers to enter private homes, to rob and steal everything in sight?" Garnet asked scornfully. "You've already taken what little we have—"

"We have requisition orders for every bit of livestock found on rebel property," he retorted, his narrowed eyes cold as steel. "*All* will be confiscated by the Government."

"Have you no honor, no decency that you would threaten a household of defenseless women with no man to protect them?" she demanded.

"Have your Rebel husband come home and protect you!"

Garnet drew in her breath at the insult and saw in an instant flash of discernment that his mean-spirited nature was a mixture of envy, hatred and revenge. Something in this man's life had formed him into this mold. She saw in his expression that woman or not, Garnet was his enemy and should be treated as such.

"Please! You are taking the food out of the mouths of little children and a sick woman!"

The men went about their despicable tasks as if they had not even heard her. One man looked over his shoulder at her and shouted an obscenity. Feeling nauseated, Garnet averted her eyes and with a great effort pulled herself away. She staggered back through the pantry and out into the hall. Carrie with Jonathan was crouched under the curve of the stairwell. She stopped there for a moment, murmuring some words of comfort or encouragement, hardly aware of what she was doing.

Then she mounted the steps, dreading what must be taking place on the second floor as she heard the heavy clump of bootsteps on the floorboards.

To her utter despair when she reached the top of the stairs, she saw the spoilers had done their work as thoroughly there as well.

They had entered every bedroom, pulling covers and linens off every bed. Nothing had been left untouched, bureau drawers yanked out, the contents overturned on the floor and tromped underfoot as the mad search went on. Curtains had been dragged down, draperies torn, armoires opened and clothes indiscriminately scattered in every direction—dresses, bonnets, cloaks and shoes tossed everywhere.

Garnet, standing in the middle of the hall, glanced down toward Sara's wing and saw Dove, with Dru in her arms, bravely guarding the door.

She heard Dove's soft, sweet voice raised as two of the soldiers advanced. "Sirs, in the name of God, I entreat you. My mother-in-law is a very sick woman, the sight of you in her private rooms could kill her! I beg you to think of your own mothers and how you would feel if they were being treated thus."

To her amazement Garnet saw the two men, even as they mumbled oaths, turn away with shamed faces and start in another direction. This time Garnet realized it was her own wing of the house to which they were heading.

With a heart-clutching sensation, she thought of that apartment she had come to as a bride, all newly decorated and furnished, with the beautiful cabbage rose wallpaper, the velvet draperies, the marble-topped tables, the bedroom with its satin quilt and lacy pillows. All her jewelry and the little gold ormulu clock and her Staffordshire dogs on the mantlepiece, the globed wax flower arrangements. . . .

She closed her eyes and drew a long, ragged breath as she heard the sound of porcelain breaking, the tinkling sound of shattering glass.

Heartsick, she turned and started back down the stairs, her knees shaking so that she had to cling to the banister. The front door had been flung open and suddenly she heard the increased sound of pounding horses' hooves. She hurried down the last few steps and ran out to the porch just in time to see soldiers coming from the stables with the six carriage horses, the four chestnuts that belonged to Mr. Montrose, the two bays for Sara's landau. But it was when she saw a trooper with her horse on a lead with Jonathan's pony behind it that she threw caution to the wind. She ran across the porch, down the steps and across the lawn and made a grab at the soldier's reins shouting, "You can't take that pony! It belongs to a little boy! I won't let you!"

The trooper looked startled at first, then a mean, vindictive expression came over to his face. "Let go my reins, woman!"

"Not the pony! You can't take it!" Garnet said dragging on the reins until the horse, tossing his head wildly, came to a stop.

Jonathan, who had followed her out to the porch, now stood at the top of the steps, sobbing and calling, "Aunt 'Net, don't let them take Bugle Boy!"

"I won't, honey!" Garnet screamed back and moved to untie the lead when all of a sudden a slicing pain snapped her head back and brought scalding tears to her eyes. The soldier had brought his crop down to hit her hands, missed, and in his swinging thrust had slashed her face. Garnet dropped the rope knotted onto Trojan Lady's lead and put a trembling hand to her cheek. It came away bloody.

"That'll teach you, you —" The trooper called her a name Garnet had never heard used in her presence. She only knew by the way it was hurled at her of its crude vulgarity. With the vicious attack, the trooper spurred his horse, jerking its reins and rode off, pulling Jonathan's fat pony after him.

Another soldier riding nearby gave a harsh laugh and shouted at Garnet, "I'd be careful if I was you, lady! This house is marked for burning! We know you've been harboring rebels! I wouldn't take no chance going to sleep too soundly tonight!"

Garnet stood there momentarily stunned, feeling the blood trickling through the fingers of the hand she held to her cheek, as the noise and loud voices of the soldiers pounding by her reverberated in her ears.

Garnet who had never been touched except in tenderness, gentleness and love, felt the excruciating pain of the lash quiver from the side of her face all down her arm. Suddenly she felt the bitter taste of nausea rise up in her and she doubled over and slowly sank onto the dusty ground.

Everything blurred before her as the pain exploded in her brain and she fought the blackness of faintness come upon her. She lowered her head and saw her blue skirt spotted with crimson.

Then Garnet felt a hard thud on her back and knew that Jonathan had run from the porch and flung himself upon her. His little arms went around her neck in a stranglehold and he was sobbing hysterically, the hot tears dampening the collar of her dress.

CHAPTER 5

"THOSE BRUTES!" Dove said over and over as she and Tilda fussed over Garnet, applying cloths wrung out in cool water to her face, which was already beginning to swell. It was so painful that Garnet could barely bear the gentle pressure of their ministrations.

Harmony stood a little apart, looking on, wringing her hands and shaking her head, making small, sympathetic noises as the other two hovered over Garnet.

"Is anyone with Mama?" Garnet asked.

"Carrie's with her." Dove replied.

"Well, don't tell her about this," Garnet said, closing her eyes and wincing as the pad Tilda was pressing against her cheek sent pain searing through her. "I'll not go up. Seeing me like this would only upset her more." She sighed, then looked at Dove and said, "But we should probably give her a double dose of laudanum tonight if what that man said is true. If they're really going to come back tonight and . . . torch the house. Perhaps that was just meant to terrorize us."

"Her supply of laudanum is getting low . . . just like everything else." Dove shook her head.

"Well, we still have camomile tea," Garnet said wearily. "Whatever else, we don't need her in hysterics."

"What about tonight?" Dove asked. "What are we going to do?"

"I don't know what we can do but be ready to leave at a minute's notice." Garnet's head ached so furiously it was difficult to think. But she knew she had to try, help Dove plan. She could count on Dove to carry out any suggestion.

Every nerve in her body seemed to be twitching. Deep within her burned a fiery anger at the outrage of the morning, but she knew she had to keep it under control, to think clearly what would be best for all the lives under her charge.

"Oh, God, what now?" she heard herself moan.

"Garnet, you need to rest for a bit now. I'll come back later and we can talk . . . decide . . ." Dove said softly. "I'll go see Mama now and check on the children. Linny is with them so they are all right for now. Except Jonathan—he's very upset about his pony."

Dove covered Garnet lightly with an afghan and tiptoed out of the room, leaving Garnet alone.

But it was impossible for Garnet to rest. She felt so helpless. What were they going to do? Without food? Without horses for transportation or for the farm work? But then what was left of the farm? The animals had been taken or killed. The fury of her hopeless dilemma swept over her and her muscles reacted, jerking spasmodically.

Unable to lie still, Garnet pulled herself up stiffly. She saw Rose's Bible that she now kept by her bedside for those sleepless nights. She groped for it, brought it up to her breast, clutching it with both hands, feeling the roughness of its blistered cover. Holding it against her, she rocked back and forth in a kind of agony. She remembered Rose saying once, "There is an answer for everything in the Bible. It wasn't just written for people living in those times—it has meaning for our lives now." Was there any meaning for what had happened to her that morning? Garnet wondered bitterly.

She placed the Bible on her lap and prayed silently: *O Father, you know I'm having a hard time believing that You really care about me, about what's going on here. I want to believe, with all my heart, I really do! I want to trust You like Rose did, only somehow, it's harder for*

*me. I thank You for what You've done for me before
now. I know You helped me that time I had to go to
Richmond, take those papers for Bryce. I know You are
helping me manage things here. But, O God, I don't
know what to do now! I am so scared. Lord, show me in
Your Word what this is all about, what I should do!*

She opened the Bible, turning the pages one by one,
until she came to Psalm 91. There her eyes rested and
she began to read.

"Oh God!" Garnet pleaded aloud. "Give me *courage!*
Whatever is ahead, whatever lies in store, don't let me
give way!"

Garnet did not realize it, but in that heart's cry, in that
act of flinging herself on His mercy and protection, she
had come the closest yet to believing God was real.

That evening as it grew dark and night approached,
struggling to mask their own fear for the sake of the
children, the women went about shuttering the windows,
bolting the doors, shoving furniture in frontof them,
leaving only one avenue of escape if the threat of burning
was carried out. This was through the pantry, out to the
breezeway that connected the kitchen to the main house.
They decided that they would bed down in the dining
room all together. The women would take turns keeping
watch while the others slept if they could.

They fed the children, dressed them in warm, outer
clothing over their nightdresses, made them beds of
quilts and pillows in the center of the room. Childlike,
Alair and Jonathan thought it an adventure and, since the
adults did not betray their own apprehensions, they were
allowed to make a game of it.

Carrie was stationed outside Sara's room in the upper
hall so that she could be alerted at a minute's notice to
help Sara out. Since she was the strongest and stoutest of
the Negro women, she could easily carry the fragile
invalid, if it came to that.

Everything was done now that could be done. To her
own surprise, Garnet heard herself say, "There is
nothing more to do now but pray."

The other women nodded. They formed a circle
around the children, who, with the innocence of child-

hood, were cuddled down and drowsy in spite of the peril that surrounded them.

"How shall we pray?" quavered Harmony.

"We'll pray the Psalms," Garnet answered with assurance unknown to her before. She got out Rose's Bible and in the flickering light from the stub of a single candle she began to read the 91st Psalm, heavily marked by Rose's hand:

> I will say of the Lord,
> The Lord is my refuge and my *fortress:* . . .
> My God, *in Him* will I *trust.* . . .

As she continued her voice grew stronger:

> Surely He shall *deliver* thee
> from the snare of the fowler. . . .
> He shall cover thee . . .
> Under His wings shalt thou trust. . . .

There was more assurance now in Garnet's reading:

> *Thou shall not be afraid*
> *for the terror by night,*

she read with great emphasis.

> Nor of the arrow that flieth by day.
> Nor of the pestilence that walketh in darkness.
> Nor of the destruction that wasteth at noonday.

Her voice broke a little at this point, and there were soft sighs, low sobs from the women kneeling with her in the shadows.

> A thousand may fall at thy side,
> Ten thousand at thy right hand;
> But *it shall not come nigh thee*.
> Only with thine eyes shalt thou behold
> And see the reward of the wicked.

Garnet swallowed thinking of what had happened to them. It certainly looked as if the victors had walked away with the spoils. She went on steadily:

Because thou hast made the Lord,
which is my refuge,
Even the Most High, thy habitation;
There shall *no evil befall thee,*
Neither shall any plague come nigh thy dwelling.
For He shall give His angels charge over thee.

A hushed quietness fell on the little group.

Suddenly a loud knocking shattered the stillness. All the women jumped. Garnet scrambled to her feet. There was a frightened moan from Harmony. The others stirred anxiously.

Garnet thought, *Oh, dear God, they've come to burn the house, to give us five minutes to get out!*

Her mind raced to Carrie keeping watch outside Sara's room. Should she send one of them to help her with Sara and have Linny get the children ready to run outside? Before she could decide what to do first, another knock came at the front door.

"Wait! Hush!" Garnet commanded the others. "Why would they just knock if they'd come to burn the house. We would have heard the horses! Maybe it's someone sent from Cameron Hall to see if we're all right, to help us. I'll go. Everyone stay just as you are. Don't wake the children. Not yet."

She took the candle and started down the dark hall toward the front door, not knowing what awaited her on the other side.

"Who is it?" she asked in a voice louder and steadier than she felt.

"Major Jeremy Devlin," came a deep, masculine voice.

Garnet held the candle higher and peered out through the glass panels on either side of the door. All she could make out was the dark outline of a tall uniformed figure. The voice came again reassuringly.

"I am alone, ma'am. There is nothing to fear, I assure you. I just want to speak with you. On my honor, ma'am."

"What do you want?" Garnet asked cautiously.

"I have come on a mission of my own as an officer and a gentleman, ma'am," was the reply.

Garnet hesitated only a minute longer, then dragged away the chest they had pulled across the door, slipped the bolt back and opened the door. In the wavering light of the candle, she could see a man, strongly built, wearing a Union officer's well-cut uniform. He bared his head and bowed politely.

"I have come to deeply apologize for the trouble, for the discourtesy with which you have been treated. The men who vandalized your home came here before I arrived at the garrison. I do not know on whose orders. However, I am here to tell you I will personally guard these premises so that your household can rest secure." At this, he saluted, turned, and marched down the porch steps. Garnet watched, amazed, as he tethered his horse, then took a place on one of the lower steps.

She closed the door, overcome with a feeling of relief and gratitude. Surely it was an answer to their prayers, a confirmation of the words David had written long ago in the Psalms they had just been reading: *My God, a constant help in time of trouble. I called to you in my distress and you heard and answered me. Blessed is the name of the Lord,* she whispered.

In the gray light of dawn Garnet got up from the floor where she had been resting and went to the window just in time to see Major Devlin mount his horse and ride off in the morning mist.

For the next two days there were no Yankee visitations. But each evening at dusk, a lone rider would appear at the bend of the driveway and take his post at the front of the house.

The household slept peacefully.

Two days later, Garnet was in the pantry helping Tilda re-sack some of the flour they had swept up from the Yankees' wanton pillage when she heard Jonathan shouting at the top of his voice.

"Aunt 'Net! Aunt 'Net! It's Bugle Boy! Some Yankee's brought him back!"

Jonathan, who had been trying to help them, dropped

the small bucket he was filling with corn meal and ran into the yard.

Garnet followed him. A blue-uniformed officer on horseback was coming up the drive, leading the trotting butterscotch colored Shetland pony toward the house. He stopped as Jonathan reached him and watched as the small boy threw his arms around the pony's neck, hugging him and saying over and over, "Bugle Boy! Oh, Bugle Boy! You're back! You've come home!"

She recognized the officer. It was Major Devlin.

Garnet picked up her skirts and hurried forward, then she stopped. Her hand automatically went to her cheek where the welt from the trooper's whip had left an ugly, red mark. It had not been visible in the dark when he had come to guard Montclair. She wondered if he had also heard of that incident.

The Major again bared his head and said quietly, "I want to apologize again for what happened. It was a shameful deed."

"Their excuse was—they said we were known to be harboring Confederate soldiers," Garnet said scornfully. "It wasn't true."

Major Devlin frowned, shook his head slightly, "An inexcusable episode. Totally without cause." He paused, then said, "Strange, but we had entirely opposite counter-intelligence that this place was a station on the Underground Railroad, assisting blacks to freedom in the North."

Bewildered by his statement, Garnet did not reply.

"This pony was brought in along with other horses conscripted for army use, but I had not had an opportunity to inspect them until this morning. When I saw him . . . I knew there was no need for him and no use to us in his acquisition. I understand he belongs to this boy."

Garnet nodded. "Thank you for returning him," she said stiffly. She felt an urge to burst out with all the other things *conscripted* by his men, but thought better of it. The less said to the enemy, the better.

It was he who seemed to linger, openly enjoying the reunion of boy and pony. His eyes resting on the two seemed to soften, "My sister has a boy about your boy's age," he remarked thoughtfully.

Garnet drew herself up, the old defiant stance, and lifted her chin proudly. "I hope he and his family have not been subjected to suffering such as we have known." Then she shrugged and added, "But then you are the victors and we the vanquished, and the fortunes of war are always weighed in the balance of the invader," she said coldly.

Major Devlin glanced away from Jonathan and regarded Garnet with a steady, direct gaze. She was taken aback by the expression of genuine regret, almost sadness, in his clear, gray eyes.

When he spoke his voice was edged with melancholy, "This War will leave no man the victor. It is a cruel travesty on the dreams our mutual forefathers dreamed for this nation. American against American, state against state, brother against brother. The wounds, both North and South, have been deep and will not soon nor easily be healed. I pray to God that this child and all the children of this land will eventually build something stronger and better over the scar."

Major Devlin made a slight bow from the waist, gave Garnet a salute at the brim of his hat, then turned his horse and cantered back down the driveway.

Garnet stood watching him until he was out of sight.

Afterward, Garnet kept thinking about what Major Devlin had said. She had not known much more than rumors about the so-called Underground Railroad. Before the War she had been too self-centered to think of anything else. Now she wondered. Could Rose have been in any way involved? One by one random thoughts began to fall into place, forming a tapestry of understanding. Rose's sympathy with the slaves: she had been secretly teaching her own servants to read and write. That had come out when the three, Tilda, Carrie and Linny, had confessed why they were all in Rose's bedroom the night of the fatal fire.

Then, how did Rose alone know about the hidden room in Jonathan's nursery? Had she held black people there and somehow sneaked them out and to freedom?

Lizzie! Garnet gasped. Had Rose even helped Lizzie escape?

Slowly the probable truth gripped Garnet, followed by

a kind of awed admiration. How daring of her! How brave to have risked so much for her convictions that slavery was wrong!

Garnet thought of those heavily underlined passages in Rose's Bible: "I can do all things through Christ which strengtheneth me." How much fragile, gentle Rose must have relied on the Word of God to give her the courage to carry out such dangerous tasks.

Regretfully, Garnet wished she had known Rose better, allowed herself to love her sooner.

Part V

MONTCLAIR

Spring, 1865

The Lord watch between me and thee, when we are absent one from the other.

Genesis 31:49

CHAPTER 1

THE FIRST WEEK OF APRIL the weather was beautiful. The
trees wore pale green halos as the delicate first foliage
began to appear. The orchards blossomed into canopies
of pink and white fairy lace. Walking through the sweet-
scented paths, Garnet breathed in the perfumed air,
relishing the beauty as if for the first time, realizing she
had taken happiness so carelessly in the past, never
knowing each day should be treasured.

That spring, bad news followed bad news. The crum-
bling of the Confederacy came as hammer blows on
heartbreak as one after the other of the strongholds fell
before the sheer numbers of the enemy that now seemed
invincible. Vicksburg, then Atlanta taken over by the
Federal forces. At Montclair, infrequent letters from
friends and relatives related the dire disasters that had
befallen those in the path of Sherman's ruthless drive to
the sea.

Although all seemed entirely lost, Cousin Nell's notes
relayed that Richmond was still putting up a gallant front.
President Davis maintaining in spite of the tragedy of the
death of his small son " little Joe" in an accident.

Then like the proverbial last straw—the word that
Charleston had surrendered, the soul of the Confederacy
broken. Where it all began, it ended.

Within days the pretense that the remnants of the Confederate Army would fight on was discarded. Lee surrendered his weary, hungry troops to Grant and the hopes of the South were finally shattered. President Davis and his Cabinet evacuated Richmond, and within forty-eight hours Richmond was occupied by Federal troops. The War was over after four endless years. On top of the dreadful defeat they suffered, the South was stunned by the shocking tidings of Lincoln's assassination. Now they girded themselves for a personal Apocalypse believing the vengeance of the North would be terrible.

Finally word reached Montclair that Leighton had died of wounds and illness in a Yankee prison hospital. Dove's brave resignation was an inspiration even as they mourned him with her.

As summer approached Garnet worried over what they would do about the acres of unplowed, unplanted fields. The field hands who had come back after being recruited by the Army showed no inclination to work, and Garnet hoped desperately Mr. Montrose would soon come home and take over some of these responsibilities. The last letter they had from him was posted in Georgia, where he had gone to oversee some of the fortification building. They knew that no one who had been connected with the Confederate government, as he had been, would be allowed to travel through "occupied territory" now without taking the oath of allegiance to the United States. Garnet was not sure the proud, stubborn Clayton Montrose would ever bow to that demand.

Men began to straggle home. Harmony got word her husband was coming and they all went to the Mayfield depot to meet him. The scene this time was a far cry from the days when they had seen their eager, youthful soldiers off to battle. Then, the air had been filled with gaiety and gallant promise.

For those at Montclair the day to day effort for survival seemed overshadowed by the new fears that sharpened their ordinary daily life. The Negroes, informed of their freedom, began to slip away, leaving work undone, fields unplowed, wandering the countryside in search of their liberators and the new life

143

promised them. The Yankee raid that had depleted their stores had not been replenished, and the gardens were still unplanted.

When Clint Chance stepped off the train, Garnet hardly recognized him as the strong, young man she had known. Harmony burst into tears at the sight of his worn, hollowed face, his shoulders sagging under the once-trim gray uniform, now torn and stained. He gathered his wife into his arms silently. As his eyes met Garnet's over her head, only she saw the utter weariness and defeat in them.

Clint and his little family left soon to go to his parents' plantation outside of Winchester, though they were uncertain as to how it had survived its Yankee occupation. Guiltily, Garnet felt no real regret at seeing them go. It meant less mouths to feed for one, and Harmony had never been any great help.

One morning soon after, they came down for breakfast and found Bessie had departed. Tilda informed them that she had packed all her things the day before and left at dawn. It was only one more incident in all the other changes of the post-War South. The same thing was happening in the households of most of the people they knew. A whole new order was being established, and no one knew exactly how it would evolve.

Then one night, toward the end of April, Garnet went to bed after a particularly wearying day. It had started raining early in the evening and it rained all night. The wind rose and the rain and wind beat upon windows, sending the boughs of the trees scraping against the house. Garnet had fallen asleep to the sound and did not know why she awakened.

Wide awake, she sat up in bed listening—for what she did not know. It was then she heard hoofbeats on the crushed shell drive below. Her heart thumped in alarm. There had been bands of renegades, stragglers, deserters from both armies seen in the vicinity over the weeks since the surrender, and she was frightened.

She got out of bed, moved cautiously over to the window and, concealing herself behind the curtain,

144

peered out into the misty night. She saw a single horseman coming slowly up the drive.

The last time Bryce was home he had taught her to use a pistol, loaded it for her and told her to keep it at her bedside at night in case she ever had to defend herself. With trembling hands Garnet picked it up, ran on tiptoe out into the hallway, then padded barefoot down the stairway across the lower hall and to the front door. She looked out one of the glass panels, holding her breath.

As the figure on horseback came nearer, Garnet stiffened. As she watched she saw the shadow of Josh, the faithful groom who had taken to sleeping on the veranda at night to protect the household. Instantly he was on his feet, rushing down the steps toward the stranger. Garnet stood frozen as Josh took hold of the horse's bridle with one hand, then used the other to support the rider's body that was slumping forward.

In the same instant she realized who it was and flung open the door, she heard Josh nearly sobbing, "Lawdy, lawdy, Miz Garnet! It's Marse Bryce!" He was staggering under the burden of the taller, heavier man. Garnet rushed to help, hardly aware of the gravel cutting into the soles of her bare feet.

Bryce gave a groan as they half-carried, half-dragged him down from the horse. Garnet saw that one arm hung useless, and his torn uniform was stiff with blood.

"Go get somebody to help!" Garnet ordered Josh. "Quick!"

The rain was soaking her, her unbound hair streamed into her face, her nightgown was clinging to her. She knelt beside Bryce, knowing they must get him into the house, tend to his wound.

Josh was back with one of the younger men, and together they picked Bryce up and carried him into the house. By this time Dove had awakened and was standing at the top of the stairs.

"It's Bryce!" Garnet told her hoarsely. "He's been hurt."

Dove ran down the steps. She took in Garnet's condition and said, "You're wet through, Garnet. Go get changed. I'll help Bryce."

Her teeth chattering from the chill, Garnet threw on

her clothes and was back downstairs in a flash. The men had laid Bryce on a sofa in the parlor, and Dove had cut away the sleeve of his coat, revealing a bullet wound in his upper arm that had splintered the bone. It had been primitively treated, for it was festering.

Dove and Garnet's eyes met in alarm.

"We'll have to go for the doctor in Mayfield tomorrow," Garnet said through stiff lips. Blood poisoning could have already started, she realized. "We'll clean it as best we can tonight and . . . pray!"

Bryce was out of his head with fever. Garnet wasn't sure whether he knew he had somehow made it home. She leaned over him to hear what he was mumbling, then straightened and nodded to Josh.

"It's his horse he's worried about. Take him out to the barn, Josh. Rub him down, see he gets some oats."

Together, Garnet and Dove cleansed and wrapped Bryce's arm, made him as comfortable as they could. They were afraid to move him until the doctor had seen the arm, afraid they might start the bleeding again, that a piece of shattered bone might pierce an artery.

Tilda, aroused by the stir, had come out from the room near the kitchen where she slept, and helped the other two women. When Dove went back to bed, Tilda remained beside Garnet in her vigil.

Josh left early the next morning and brought back a young doctor recently paroled, who had served as an Army surgeon in Richmond. He examined Bryce immediately.

Garnet took one look at Dr. Myles' face and a cold certainty wrenched her heart. He had dressed Bryce's wound, left powders for the fever, but there was something in his eyes that betrayed the professional cheerfulness of his voice.

When he said gravely, "It's a matter of time," she was not exactly sure whether he meant "until he's well" or "until he dies."

"I've seen many men in worse condition recover, Mrs. Montrose," he told her. "Your husband has suffered from exposure and the wound has gone untended who knows how long . . . but with good care. . . ."

Dr. Myles repacked his bag with a sigh. Something in

his voice chilled Garnet's heart, something in his eyes betrayed a cold certainty when he added, "Only time will tell—"

She thrust back the fear that rushed up chokingly inside her. In its place came a fierce determination. She would not let Bryce die. He couldn't die! Not before she had a chance to show him how much she had changed, how much she regretted her selfishness. Please God, not before she had a chance to make up to him for all that she had not done that might have made him happier.

Garnet knew it was wrong to bargain with God, but in spite of that, desperate prayers began to pour out of her as she vowed to do everything in her power to nurse Bryce back to health.

There was something redemptive in each task Garnet set herself to, as if in a way she was doing penance for all the wrongs she had done Bryce. The first and worst was marrying him when she had not really loved him, depriving him of a wife who would have loved him more completely. She hoped somehow she would be forgiven for that sin even though she found it hard to forgive it in herself.

She found a kind of exaltation in the very menialness of all she did, serving him in the necessities without which he would not have been comfortable, nor be healed and eventually recover—as if in doing these things, she was compensating for all the times she had not treated him with kindness or consideration.

"Thank God, he did not die!" she whispered to herself as she hovered over his bed, washing his wasted frame, turning the hot fever-warmed pillow, gently combing his thick wavy hair.

Whenever he opened his eyes, hazy and drugged with fever, he seemed surprised to see her. He murmured something unintelligible and weakly held her hand. She had to bend low to hear the words of gratitude he whispered.

She felt ashamed. She deserved no gratitude. She only wanted him to live. But as the days passed and there was no improvement, Garnet grew frantic.

Word had gone out to the quarters, and the few remaining Negroes gathered in little clusters under the bedroom window each morning to see if Marse Bryce had lived through the night. Garnet would go to the window and raise her hand and nod, and they would move away slowly, murmuring among themselves, shaking their heads. Bryce was well-loved among the Montrose people. She had never heard him say an unkind word to any of them.

Mom Becca, Bryce's old nurse, long crippled with arthritis, had not worked for years. She spent her days sitting either by the fire in her little cabin or in the sun in front of it. Now she daily shuffled laboriously up the stairway of the big house and took a place outside the bedroom door, where "ma baby" lay nearly unconscious most of the time.

One day, late in the afternoon, Garnet was sitting alone beside the bed and Bryce opened his eyes, for once seeming clear and lucid. He moistened his cracked lips, raised one hand weakly and motioned her closer. She leaned down to hear what he wanted to say.

"We're two of a kind, darlin'." His fingers curled around her hand. "We thought our world was the only one." He shook his head, his sad gaze upon her. "It isn't, you know. You're finding that out, too, my poor little Garnet." His eyes widened, grew bright with tears.

"People like us are a dying breed. Nobody out in the real world gives a tinker's dam about us. They call us the idle rich. Only a handful of us are left even in the South. We lived in a dream. Even thought war was some kind of glorious game. But it wasn't." His eyes grew wild, his grasp on her hand tightened painfully. "It was *hell* !"

"I saw it . . . it was hell! I believe in hell, Garnet. I didn't always before, but now I know what it must be like. . . ."

"Please, Bryce, save your strength, honey," she pleaded.

"I just want to know it was worth it," he groaned.

"Yes, it was worth it . . ." she said, frightened that she might not be able to control him. "Lie back now, honey. . . ." She smoothed the sheet soothingly.

"Life is precious, Garnet. I've seen so much wasted."

Garnet began to stroke his hand. She wished Tilda

would come in so they could give him one of those powders the doctor had left.

His head moved restlessly on the pillow, then his eyes closed wearily. "You don't understand . . . but how could you?"

"Please, Bryce, don't get so excited, honey, it's bad for you."

Bryce struck the mattress weakly with a clenched fist. Two tears rolled down from under his closed eyelids over the hollowed cheek.

He seemed to fall into a agitated slumber after awhile and Garnet, looking down at him, tried to recall the dashing young officer in his slouch hat, his fresh uniform and shiny boots who had ridden away through the gates of Montclair four years ago accompanied by his black body servant and two fine horses. The picture faded as she tried to bring it back, much as if it had never been.

She couldn't think about the past. She must think of the future. *That's the only way I can keep from falling apart*, Garnet told herself, willing the weak grieving part of herself into iron.

The only way I can stand what's happened is to believe that things will be better. I will be better, too. I'm better than I used to be. She looked down at the gray, thin face on the pillow. When Bryce was well, he would see how she had changed.

Not that she didn't still have a temper or get easily annoyed by stupidity or slowness. But that was mostly because she had discovered she had a brain and could often see better ways to get things done. She'd had to change these last years. But she wanted Bryce to benefit from those changes. More than anything else, she wanted the chance to be a better wife to him, better than the old Garnet would have even chosen to be.

But soon Garnet realized she would never have that chance. The doctor's next visit confirmed her worst fears. "No need for me to come any more unless there is some crisis." By that, she knew he was telling her there was no hope.

Bryce slept more and more, waking for brief intervals. Garnet left him only to bathe, rest, or eat something to keep up her strength. Always the bulky black figure at the door remained. Every once in awhile, Mom Becca would give a heavy sigh and say mournfully, "Glory, glory, sweet Jesus."

One evening, Garnet was alone with Bryce, Tilda having gone for a little rest and Mom Becca persuaded to lie down. Sitting in the shadows with only the dim light of one lamp, Garnet became conscious Bryce was stirring. She went at once to him, bending near.

He opened his eyes, tried to smile. She leaned down, took his hand, pressed it to her breast, trying to hear the hoarse whispered words,

"Thank you," he said.

Garnet's heart contracted.

"There's nothing to thank me for, Bryce," she protested. Inside she grieved, inside she confessed *I never loved you the way I should have, or appreciated you. I loved another man most of our marriage*.

But Garnet knew better than to ease her own conscience by unburdening her guilty secret to a dying man. It was too late to do anything but give him comfort as he slipped away. His voice was weak, but she bent close and heard him say, "Rose was right, you know. About life—and after. I'm sure of it now. . . ." His voice faded away.

At first, Garnet did not understand what he meant about Rose. Then she remembered Rose had believed in "a place of beauty, light and peace" after death. A sob pressed against Garnet's throat as she thought of how she had read to Rose from her Bible the last day of her life.

Garnet turned her head and saw lying on the bedside table the small worn black leather New Testament and Psalms Rose had given Bryce before he went to War. Somehow it had survived the months of battle, the weather, the rough riding Bryce had been through. They had found it in the inside pocket of his uniform jacket when they had cut it off him.

Now she reached for the little book and asked him, "Would you like me to read something for you, honey?"

His eyes were closed. *He's sinking fast*, something warned her. Still holding Bryce's hand, Garnet fumbled through the pages of the book with the other and found a well-marked passage in Psalms. She wondered how often Bryce must have read this by the light of a campfire to have underlined it so many times.

Slowly, haltingly she began to read:

The Lord is my strength and song,
And is become my salvation. . . .

The Lord has chastened me sorely:
But He has not given me over unto death.

Open to me the gates of righteousness:
I will go into them,
And I will praise the Lord:
This is the gate of the Lord,
Into which the righteous shall enter.

I will praise thee:
For thou hast heard me,
And art my salvation.

There was a sound from Bryce. Garnet stopped reading, sank to her knees beside the bed. Bryce was trying to tell her something.

"You've been so good to me."

"Not half good enough." she said brokenly. "I have not been what you deserved."

"You've been all I've ever wanted." he said.

She held him in her arms until his head dropped to one side and she knew with a sudden sense of abandonment that he was gone.

Garnet did not know how long she knelt there, feeling the weight of Bryce against her shoulder. After awhile she laid his head gently on the pillow and got up.

She moved slowly, stiffly, over to the window and looked down into the garden where the rose bushes were in full bloom, so heavy they drooped their heads and fell in a flutter of petals onto the ground. No one had bothered to pick them, for the whole household had been suspended during the last few days as "Marse Bryce" lay dying.

"He's gone," Tilda had said, and so was Leighton, and her father, Stewart and Rose, gone *where?* The tears she had held back so long began to flow now as she thought in anguish what Bryce had said . . . "I'm sure of it now. . . ." Garnet leaned against the window frame. She felt a bittersweet pain. Bryce had gone, left her and now he knew, and she did not.

He had spoken that day his mind was so clear of "wasted lives." Their life together had been wasted. It was true even as she knew it was useless to regret. He had also said, "We're two of a kind." That also was true. Headstrong, reckless, spoiled—but they had both grown and they might have become more, much more together, given time. They might have one day had children together, Garnet mourned, and she put her head into her hands and sobbed out her remorse.

But Garnet had not yet shed all her tears.

CHAPTER 2

ONLY HIS SON'S DEATH and funeral would have ever induced Clay Montrose to take the despised oath of allegiance in order to come home in time to bury Bryce.

War had taken its toll on the sturdy, youthful looking man. The twinkle was gone from his eyes, the spring from his step. The uprightness of his proud carriage was bowed now beneath the weight of the years of suffering.

Garnet watched his approach from the parlor windows, saw him mount the veranda steps with a kind of leaden weariness. She saw him stop short at seeing the crêpe-hung front door, throwing one arm up in front of him as if warding off a blow. She turned away and walked into the hall to meet him.

A small band of neighbors and friends gathered in the other parlor to mourn the second Montrose son to fall in the service of the Confederacy. Only the year before, they had been present at her father's funeral at Cameron Hall.

Garnet stood with her father-in-law to receive their condolences, to hear people remark in amazement at her calm and strength.

In truth, Garnet herself was awed by the deep peace she felt. Maybe the full impact of Bryce's death and the grief would come later, but now she was in a state of transcendent thankfulness. Bryce was beyond pain and the bitterness she saw in some of the other eyes that gazed into her own. It seemed to her in these last weeks that she and Bryce had been closer than they had ever been, that she had been given a priceless gift.

In the past two days her mind had been cleared into a startling truth that stunned her. She knew now that what she had imagined love to be did not exist. It had all been an illusion. Like her love for Malcolm. It seemed to her now some kind of sickness, a shallow hope without foundation that had bred within her jealousy and bitterness, near hatred for someone innocent—Rose! More than that, it had led her into a loveless marriage. Another sin against an innocent person—Bryce!

Now, she knew with a knowledge born of grief and loss what love really was. She had learned it in the days she had nursed Bryce, praying for forgiveness. The old Garnet would never have imagined that one day she would sit beside a man, broken in body, mind and spirit, and know the true, full meaning of love.

For weeks after Bryce's death, Garnet could not sleep at night. She paced the floor restlessly, her mind as wide awake as if it were morning. Sometimes she slept for a few hours toward dawn on the chaise lounge in her dressing room. Somehow she could not bring herself to sleep in the bed Bryce had died in, the one they had shared through their tempestuous marriage.

She did not know what to do. The future loomed ahead in bleak uncertainty. In a prostrate South few knew how to face the changed order.

One of those was Clay Montrose. His whole world had disappeared, and he did not know how to put the pieces back together. Once authoritative and decisive, he was now totally frustrated. Only a remnant of blacks remained from his hundreds of slaves, too few to restore the farmlands to complete productivity. There were new laws that had to be observed dealing with former servants, papers to fill out, forms to be filed.

Observing her father-in-law's changed persona, Garnet gradually came out of her own grief-stricken cocoon and tried to comfort him. "When Malcolm comes home, things will be different, Father Montrose. He'll help you sort things out, get started again. . . ."

Clay swore, scowled, walked over to his desk, the one that had been battered and vandalized by the Yankee invasion of Montclair, took out a letter and shook it at her.

"Malcolm won't be coming home, Garnet. We got this letter from Illinois a few days ago. I didn't want to tell you right away because I knew you thought any day. . . . Well, he won't. He's going West. Here—you can read it for yourself." He handed her the two sheets of thin paper, bearing Malcolm's familiar handwriting.

The first few paragraphs told them sparingly of the horrors of the place where he had been imprisoned since his capture at Gettysburg, of having to sleep on blankets in which some poor soul had just died of smallpox and how, by some miracle, he had escaped the illness.

At first, he had hoped to be exchanged, but then they moved him to another prison. There he had tried to smuggle out letters, but never knew if they had been received or not. They had not. His hopes of being exchanged were dashed when the new ruling came through that only men too weakened by illness or injury again would be released.

Garnet's eyes flew over the pages until she came to this part. "I have become friends with a fellow prisoner. He is from Texas—no wife or family—and we have become close companions. It is his plan that has caught my imagination, given me the hope I had almost lost in these dreadful years. We are going together to California.

"I cannot bear the thought of returning to a devastated land, a defeated South, everything I loved laid waste, destroyed. It is not impossible, I am told, that in the gold fields of California there are limitless veins of gold and other precious metals and ore running through the hills, riches to make a man wealthy, there for the taking. Any man with enough determination, strength and courage can make his fortune in a matter of months. If this is true, I can come back to Virginia a rich man, able to restore Montclair to its original splendor, restock our stables, replant and reap the harvest. I will not come back until I can do this. I will not come back a beaten man.

155

"I trust, until that happy day, my little son Jonathan will understand. That he will be proud of his father. It was Rose's wish that, after the War, he would go to see his Meredith relatives in Massachusetts. This request should be honored. I give my permission. I will let you know where I am and where you can write me as soon as Jack and I are settled somewhere. With dearest love to you, my parents, to the others at Montclair. . . ."

Silently Garnet handed the letter back to Mr. Montrose.

"We Southern men were not prepared for ruin," he said morosely.

How ironic, Garnet mused, another lingering hope shattered. For she had to admit that it had occurred to her that now that both she and Malcolm were free, there might have been a chance for them in the future. But now that had dissolved like all her other childish dreams. Even what gratitude Malcolm might feel for her in caring for his mother, his child, his home during these years, was a poor substitute for the love she had longed for—

Instinctively, Garnet straightened her shoulders as if steeling herself for yet another loss. She had lost so many whom she loved in such quick succession. This little boy was all she had left to lose.

Within weeks the letter from John Meredith came. Having anticipated yet dreaded it, Garnet opened it reluctantly. As she did, she could hear the sound of children's laughter outside—Jonathan and little Druscilla playing tag under the trees. She dragged her eyes back to the finely-scripted letter and read:

It was my dead sister's earnest request and deepest wish that in the event of her or her husband's death, their son should be sent to us to raise as our own child. In her letter written to both my sister and me shortly after she received word that Captain Montrose was missing, presumed dead, she told us she had made her wishes clear in a letter, witnessed and signed and placed in an envelope to be opened after her passing, if such a sad event were to occur. Which in spite of her youth the tragedy of Fate brought to pass—to all our sorrow.

156

Now that the calamitous War which has divided our country these past four years is at last over, I am able to communicate with you, my dear Mrs. Montrose, and convey my intention to carry out my dead sister's wishes. Rose spoke of you so lovingly in her letters to us, and I trust you returned her sisterly regard for you and are as anxious as we are to fulfill her last wishes.

I will soon be relieved of my duties here in Washington, and will be returning to civilian life shortly. If you could arrange to bring young Jonathan to Richmond, I can meet you there.

His Grandfather Meredith, his great-aunt Vanessa, my wife Frances and I are all looking forward to meeting our nephew whom we have not seen since he was an infant and to welcoming00im into our home and hearts.

> Yours most sincerely,
> John Meredith,
> Major, U.S.A.

Reading it over, Garnet tried to imagine the haughty bearing, the cold New Englander, the arrogant Army officer who was Rose's brother. The handwriting was of an educated man, a Harvard man like Malcolm, she thought bitterly . . . if Malcolm had never gone North to college, he would never have met Rose Meredith, and she would never be facing the dreadful parting before her.

Garnet folded up the letter and put it in her apron pocket, then looked out the window again.

Every time she looked at Jonathan, she saw Malcolm. He was a handsome little boy, small and quick, perfectly coordinated.

He had dark hair like his father's but his eyes were rich brown like Rose's. His skin was tanned to a golden brown after running barefoot in as few clothes as possible all through the spring, which had been early and hot this year.

Sometimes when he came running in for a drink of water, out of breath, laughing with his small, white teeth showing, his head back, his dark curls damp and tousled, Garnet could not resist snatching him up for a quick hug.

Garnet fought back the rush of anger, the resentment that flooded her, the renewal of heartbreak that cut like broken glass inside her. Biting her lip, she turned abruptly away from the window, the sight and sound of the laughing children.

It wouldn't hurt to wait awhile before telling Jonathan, Garnet decided. A few days' delay—what would it matter? They would have him the rest of his life. Why shouldn't she hold on a little longer to what should have been hers?

Two weeks later Garnet, with Jonathan, waited tensely in the lobby of the Washington hotel where she had arranged to meet John Meredith. When a tall, dark-haired man approached them, Garnet's first thought was, *Thank goodness he's not wearing a Yankee uniform!* That would have scared Jonathan right away and started them off on the wrong foot.

John Meredith was an impressive-looking man, well-dressed, serious of expression. The only resemblance he bore to Rose was his eyes—deep brown, heavily lashed for a man. And, as they rested on Jonathan, they softened noticeably.

Garnet felt Jonathan's little hand tighten in her own as the huge man approached them. She leaned down and whispered, "This is your Uncle John, honey, your mama's brother."

John Meredith halted in front of them, then knelt so that his face was on the level of the child's, his eyes looking directly into the boy's.

"Hello Jonathan." John Meredith's voice was deep, masculine, but with a gentle intonation. He held out one large hand and offered it to him. Jonathan waited a full minute then hesitantly put his small, chubby hand out and let John Meredith cover it with his. He began to speak very gently to Jonathan then.

"Jonathan, your mother was my little sister and I loved her very much and I love you, too. Not just because you're part of her, but because you're *you*. We're going to get to know each other. I'm going to take you to all the places your mama knew when she was growing up. We'll go fishing and when it snows and the river freezes, I'll teach you to ice skate. You'd like that, wouldn't you?"

Jonathan nodded, his eyes beginning to shine.

"There are two other people who loved your mama very much too. Her father, your Grandfather Meredith, and your mama's Aunt Vanessa. They've been waiting so long to meet you. Wouldn't you like to go with me to see them? They live where your mama lived when she was a little girl."

Again Jonathan nodded eagerly.

John Meredith continued to talk to Jonathan in a low, gentle voice. The little boy seemed fascinated that this big, grown-up man was giving him all this attention. He had not been around many men in his short lifetime. His memory of his own father was dim, fading more and more with every day that passed. The men who had been in and out of Montclair during the War, had played with him, teased him and tossed him into the air, tousled his head, and called him a "good little soldier." But they, too, had come and gone quickly and left no more than a fleeting impression. Now all Jonathan's focus was concentrated on this tall, gentle-voiced man, his eyes riveted on John Meredith's face, nodding every once in awhile as his uncle continued to talk. There seemed to be a total acceptance of this person who only minutes before had been a stranger.

Then, without a word to her or a look back, Jonathan went with John Meredith a little apart from Garnet, to sit together on the bench across from her.

Jonathan seemed completely absorbed in all John Meredith was telling him.

Garnet watched in resentful surprise. How quickly John Meredith had gained the child's confidence. Her immediate reaction was a kind of stunned realization that the man and boy had become friends within a few minutes. The saying "blood is thicker than water" flashed through Garnet's mind, and she thought perhaps there was some truth to that. Maybe there was an invisible bond that flowed as soon as it was activated by such a meeting.

As she watched from a distance, another emotion took the place of that first sting of hurt. It was joy, not unmixed with sorrow. She had seen the man reach out to the child with tenderness and love and the special affection given to those who are particularly dear by kinship. Garnet felt a surge of gratitude, for Jonathan's sake, that he was to have a new family who cared deeply for him, who could give him all the things neither the Montroses nor she could give him now—a comfortable home, material security, a good education. All the things Jonathan would need to grow up into a fine, outstanding, educated man and take his rightful place in life. In a defeated, impoverished South, orphaned and with an inheritance now ravished beyond restoration, Jonathan could have none of this if he remained in Virginia.

But even though her mind confirmed this truth, deep within her was resentment that, through pure weight of force, the Merediths were in a position to do more for this dearly beloved child who was so much a part of her now that he might have been born to her.

But as John Meredith led Jonathan back, and they stood before her, hand-in-hand, Garnet knew this was the best possible thing for the child.

"Well, I think it's time to go now," John Meredith was saying. "We have a train to catch. Say goodbye to your Aunt Garnet now, Jonathan," he directed gently.

Garnet folded Jonathan into her arms, struggling against the dreadful ache in her throat as she nestled her face into the thick dark curls, feeling the warmth of his small, sturdy body against her breast, the scent of his fresh-washed hair, the starchy smell of his shirt collar, and newness of his cotton suit. She kissed his cheek, then cupping his rosy little face in both her hands, she looked long into those beautiful, brown eyes now dancing with excitement.

"We're going on the *cars*, Auntie 'Net!" he exclaimed.

"I know, Jonathan!" Garnet replied, holding herself rigidly so as not to give way to the crowding tears.

She stood watching them, the tall man and the little boy, as they walked away from her, her hands clenched so tightly she felt her nails bite into the soft flesh of her palms. Just before they went down the steps, Jonathan turned and waved once—then he was gone.

Garnet had been back at Montclair less than a week when she faced another parting. Dove was taking Druscilla and going to Savannah.

"Maybe I'll be back, Garnet," Dove told her. "It's just that I haven't seen my relatives there since . . . since I lost Leighton . . . since the War." she sighed. "Montclair doesn't really seem my home any more. It never really did. Mr. Montrose had promised Lee property of our own, you know, but now . . ." She shrugged. "The only real family I have is in Savannah, although there's not much there either."

"There's my mother here," Garnet reminded her. She had come to love her sister-in-law dearly, and little Dru.

"Cousin Kate is wonderful and I love her, but she has all she can manage herself now, with Rod still recovering from his wounds and sickness, and that big place. . . ." Dove paused and her delicate face took on a determination as she said, "I've got to find my own way, learn to support myself and my daughter." She turned to Garnet and in her eyes Garnet saw a new strength. "We women of the South are survivors, Garnet. We've come through all this with more courage than anyone ever gave us credit for, but we have to find new ways of dealing with things as they are now."

Before Dove left she hugged Garnet and said tremulously with tears brightening her eyes, "I may be back, Garnet. Let's not say goodbye!" she smiled.

After they were gone Montclair seemed achingly empty, filled with the ghosts of the children who used to make the house ring with happy voices, laughter and the sound of running feet.

With Dove's going, Garnet had to fight a paralyzing apathy. She knew what Dove had said about them being survivors was true and she felt she should be getting on with her own life. But what could she do? The Montroses depended on her more and more. There was no one else to take over the responsibility of the house, the few remaining servants, to try to direct what little farming was being done now.

It seemed ironic that she should be the one who at long last was Mistress of Montclair. But how different from the way she had once dreamed it would be.

Then she received another unexpected jolt, another parting.

Garnet was sitting at the window of her room, staring vacantly out past the orchards to the river, when a tap at her half-open door made her turn to see Tilda standing there.

She was neatly dressed in gray cotton, a shawl around her shoulders. Instead of a bandana tied around her head, she wore a broad-brimmed straw hat. In one hand she had a large cloth-covered bundle, tied and knotted; in the other, a lidded split-oak basket.

"What is it, Tilda?" Garnet asked.

"Miz Garnet, I jes—kin I speak to you fo' a minute, ma'am?" The tone of voice was hesitant.

"Of course, Tilda, come on in," A queer little tingle of awareness tensed Garnet for the encounter.

Tilda set down her bundle and basket, advancing into the room, both her hands twisted nervously in front of her.

"I jes came to say I wuz goin'."

"Going where, Tilda?"

"Goin' No'th, ma'am. My Jeems is in Philadelphia since he went dere afta de War, and he done sent fo me to come. Sent me the car fare to take the train." Tilda lifted her head proudly.

"To *Philadelphia!*" exclaimed Garnet. "You don't want to go way up there where you don't know anybody, do you? Philadelphia's a big city. Does Jeems have a place for you to live? What will you do there?"

Tilda shook her head. "I doan know fo shure, Miz Garnet. But I jes knows I has to go. We is free now, Miz Garnet. I neber been nowhere 'cepn on dis here plantation. I wuz born here, lived here all my life. I gots to have ma chanct. My chillen has got to hab theirs. I mean fo them to grow up free."

Garnet stared at the black woman she had come to know, come to depend on through all that had happened in the last four years. She felt compassion, knowing Tilda did not realize what might lie ahead of her once she left Montclair. At the same time she had to admit she felt a stirring of resentment as well. Tilda was leaving, and that meant she would not be here when Garnet needed her.

But who could blame her? I'd leave if I could, Garnet sighed.

"Well, Tilda, all I can say is I hope you know what you're doing. I'd like to give you something to help you on your way, but I don't have any money." She threw out her hands, palms up.

"I knows, Miz Garnet. Jeems sent me 'nuf fo the trip." she did not add it was United States Government money. All the paper money the Montroses had now was the worthless Confederate issued kind.

Suddenly Garnet felt a desolate sensation to realize she might never see this strong, kind, black woman again, another link in the old life.

"I hate to see you leave, Tilda," she said at last.

"Well, Miz Garnet, Miz Rose taught us that we is all equal in de Lawd's sight and now de *law* sez we free jest lak ebryone else. 'Sides that, she taught me that iffen the Bible is right and we seek it, we shall know de Truf and de Truf shall set us free. I gotta seek it. Truf and Freedom. Gotta find out if what de Yankees promised is de Truf and black folks is free up No'th."

Garnet felt a tightness in her throat and chest. Tilda had been so faithful—like a rock when the children were so ill. When Bryce came home to die, she had nursed him as tenderly as if he had been her own. Impulsively Garnet got to her feet and went over to where Tilda stood and embraced her.

As the two women clung to each other, black and white, their tears poured unchecked. They knew that neither time nor distance could sever the bond that united them. They had both been born and reared in Virginia, their roots went deep in the same soil; they had been through the desert of the War together, shared its suffering and its sorrows. Though mistress and slave, they were both women and they knew that in Jesus *there was neither slave nor freeman,* but only God's beloved children.

Part VI

CAMERON HALL AND MONTCLAIR

1868-1870

And now, Lord, what wait I for? My hope is in Thee . . .
Psalm 39:7

CHAPTER 1

To GARNET'S SURPRISED DELIGHT, in a matter of weeks Dove returned.

As they hugged and laughed and cried, Dove told her, "It just didn't seem like home to me any more, Garnet! I guess Virginia is where I belong. I feel closer to Leighton here."

Dove had also come back with an idea. It came about when Dove considered answering an ad for a governess. Drawn by the mild climate, floods of affluent Northerners had begun visiting Mayfield during the winter, bringing their children.

It was then then she suggested to Kate and Garnet the possibility of opening a day and boarding school at Cameron Hall. Cameron Hall, because it had been used as a temporary headquarters for the Union officers when Mayfield was briefly in Federal hands, had not suffered the vandalism of many other beautiful homes in the area. With its large double bedrooms, it would be perfect to accommodate boarders. Together, the three could offer a curriculum to suit Northerners who admired the Southern way of life and the models of culture and gentility they had seen there.

Kate responded with enthusiasm and Garnet, eager for

anything that might supplement their meager finances, quickly fell in with the plans.

Dove, who had been educated in a convent finishing school in New Orleans taught by French nuns, instructed in French, needlework, calligraphy; Kate held classes in literature, drawing and painting, deportment; Garnet taught dancing, botany and supervised the business affairs. Next year, they were planning to have horses and Rod would instruct the young ladies in the equestrian arts.

In less than two years the success of the Cameron Hall School for Young Ladies had exceeded their wildest imagination, with a waiting list of students seeking admission.

Garnet was thinking about this surprising turn of events and fortune, on a June day in 1868 as she prepared to ride over to Cameron Hall for the commencement program.

Many of the wealthy Northern parents would be there to observe the transformation of their daughters into ladies, molded by the gentle atmosphere of Southern aristocracy.

She wanted to look especially elegant today and, as she leaned toward the oval mirror of her dressing table, she searched her reflection as if looking at a portrait of someone she had known long ago.

The changes of the past five years were not apparent to others, perhaps, but Garnet herself was sharply aware of them. Examining her image closely, she noticed the fine lines around her eyes. She turned her head this way and that, stroking her still-firm neck and chin with her fingers. Tentatively she touched her hair, which had lost some of its coppery gold, darkening into a burnished auburn. Well, at least, she had not, in spite of everything she had been through, turned prematurely gray like poor Dove, Garnet thought with some satisfaction. Her skin was still clear and her teeth still nice and what else could one hope for at twenty-eight? she demanded of her mirrored self.

Garnet still lived at Montclair and drove over to Cameron Hall three times a week to give her classes. She would have to leave soon as it took a good forty-five minutes in her buggy with her old mare.

Regarding herself in the mirror, she frowned. Her outfit lacked something, she thought. A brooch? Her mother's cameo, maybe. She opened the top bureau drawer and took out the small velvet pouch in which she kept the few family heirlooms that had not been sold or bartered for the necessities. As she moved it from its resting place on the small pile of lace-edged handkerchiefs, her fingers felt the rim of a small frame and she drew out the hidden daguerreotype and gazed at it for a long time.

"*Oh, Malcolm!*" she sighed. *Where are you? What has happened to you? Why don't you write?*"

She continued to look at that once-beloved face. But now she could hardly remember how he moved or spoke or laughed. Malcolm had become part of her past. She remembered how sick with rage she had been when she had heard of Malcolm's engagement to Rose Meredith, and how that rage had poisoned her life for so long. Now she felt another kind of rage as she gazed at Malcolm's picture. Why didn't he let them know where he was? She thought of Sara, slowly sinking into premature senility, mourning her two dead sons, grieving the loss of her favorite one, Malcolm. A cold dread overlapped Garnet's frustrated anger. Maybe Malcolm was dead, too. They had heard of the violence in the gold fields, of claim jumping or murders of miners who struck it rich then were never heard of again. Malcolm had gone to recoup his family's fortunes. But had he lost his life in the pursuit of such a far-fetched hope?

Garnet put the little picture back and shoved the drawer shut. Whatever had happened to Malcolm, she could not think about it now. Living in the past was a terrible trap. Garnet had seen too many people around here do that. She must think about only today.

"Miss Garnet, ma'am."

Garnet whirled around at the sound of Carrie's soft voice, coming from the bedroom doorway.

"Dey's a gen'leman here to see you. He axed to speak to de lady ob de house."

Garnet picked up the card on the small silver tray Carrie was holding out to her.

Puzzled, she read the name: JEREMY DEVLIN.

"Jeremy Devlin?" she repeated out loud. "Who could it be?"

Then she concluded that perhaps he was the father of one of their girls. But why would he come here to Montclair instead of to Cameron Hall?

Garnet went down the curving stairway, her hand sliding on the polished balustrade, which still bore the scars of saber marks from the days the Yankees had stormed Montclair.

Through the open front door she saw a tall, elegantly dressed man standing in the shadows of the veranda columns. She paused for a moment at the bottom of the steps. There was something vaguely familiar about the figure—something in the set of the shoulders, the shape of his head. Garnet walked slowly forward.

At the door she stopped again. Putting one graceful hand on the frame, she spoke, "You wished to see me?"

At the sound of her low, melodious question, the man turned around and Garnet's brows drew together in a frown. Who was this man? There was something about him. . . .

"Mrs. Montrose?" he bowed courteously. "Jeremy Devlin." he introduced himself although she was still holding his card in her hand. "I have taken the liberty of calling without first sending a note requesting permission. I hope you will forgive my presumption, however. . . . I had to come."

Intrigued but still mystified, Garnet asked, "But why? How? I do not believe we have ever met, have we? Perhaps it is my mother-in-law or my sister-in-law you wished to see?" Her voice faded and she instinctively shook her head. The memory was still annoyingly elusive. Perhaps he was one of the high-spirited young officers she had danced with or flirted with during that first winter of the War in Richmond, in that brief, season of gaiety and optimism and frivolity. And yet this man had a Northern accent. Who could he be?

Involuntarily Garnet stepped back, aghast. Surely this mild-spoken, graciously mannered gentleman could not have been one of those rude invaders who had terrorized them during that ruthless raid! Then, *in an instant, she knew who he was*. The gallant officer who had volunteered to guard their house and property, who had returned Jonathan's pony! Of course, *Major Jeremy Devlin*.

Garnet shook her head. "It is *you* who must forgive *me*. We have never forgotten your kindness. It's just that . . ."

He held up one hand to halt her apology.

"Please! My coming like this might even have revived painful memories. For that I am truly sorry." He gestured with one hand to the flower-strewn yard. Spring had come late and so in June Montclair was in full bloom, yellow daffodils and iris in a variety of blues, purples, pale lavender spread a magnificent carpet of color, as well as the rhododendrons and azaleas. "I always remembered this place as being so beautiful. I had to come back and assure myself that it was still here, that it had not been destroyed. . . ." An expression of concern cast a shadow on his handsome face, a catch in his voice made it falter.

"Somehow Montclair has managed to survive . . . even the Yankee army," Garnet replied, with an edge of bitterness in her tone. But her inborn good manners caused her to make a quick change of subject diverting it from that dangerous trend. "—although not too well, I'm afraid." She glanced at the weatherbeaten siding where the paint was peeling and the mildew had settled around the base of the porch posts. "So much needs doing but there's no . . ." she stopped herself before she had said *there's no money, no help and no way to pay them if you could get help*. She certainly did not want to flaunt their poverty in front of this obviously wealthy Yankee stranger. She asked quickly, "What brings you to Virginia now, Mr. Devlin? Not just curiosity surely?"

Jeremy Devlin gave a rueful smile.

"Besides being haunted by a lovely Southern mansion? Yes, Mrs. Montrose, I confess there were extenuating reasons for my being in this part of the country just now. I accompanied my sister who has come to collect her daughter attending Cameron Hall Academy."

170

Garnet gave a little gasp. "Your niece attends Cameron Hall? What is her name?"

"Malissa Bennett."

"Malissa! A really delightful girl!" smiled Garnet.

It was Devlin's turn to look surprised.

"You know Malissa?" he asked.

Garnet nodded.

"In fact, she is one of my favorite students."

"*Students?*"

Garnet could not help laughing at Devlin's expression.

"Yes. You see, Mr. Devlin, my sister-in-law and I along with my mother, Mrs. Cameron, run the school at Cameron Hall, which was my childhood home."

"But I thought this ... Montclair ... was your home."

"It was, after my marriage and during the War. My husband's parents still live here."

"And your son ... your little boy?" Devlin asked.

"My son?" Garnet shook her head. Then, with sudden awareness, she explained, "Oh, Jonathan is not mine. He is my nephew. My husband's brother's child."

"I see." Devlin hesitated a moment. "Your husband—"

"Is dead," Garnet finished for him. "Captured. Wounded. Killed." The words came out in staccato.

"I'm sorry." Devlin looked truly distressed.

The awkward moment stretched between them, then Garnet said smoothly. "You really must excuse me, Mr. Devlin. I have to leave in a very short time to get over to Cameron Hall before the program begins. I hope you are planning to attend? I'm sure Malissa would be disappointed if you weren't there."

As if he had been too abruptly brought back to the present, Jeremy Devlin took a second to reply. "Yes, indeed, I wouldn't miss it." He hesitated a little longer, then said, "Again, I beg your forgiveness for my intrusion today ... perhaps it was wrong of me to come, to stir up unpleasant memories. . . ."

"Not at all, Mr. Devlin. It gave me the opportunity to thank you again for the service you rendered us during a very ... difficult time. I remember especially your

171

extraordinary kindness in bringing Bugle Boy back to Jonathan.''

Devlin started to leave and then, halfway down the porch steps, he turned and smilingly asked, ''How is Jonathan? I imagine he has grown into quite a lad.''

Garnet's face must have shown the sadness caused by the long separation from the child she loved so much.

''He is with his mother's family in Massachusetts now. I haven't seen him in nearly three years,'' she said, and in spite of herself, her voice shook.

''I'm sorry,'' Devlin said, shaking his head. ''Again I seem to have brought up a painful subject. Dare I ask your forgiveness once more?''

Not trusting herself to answer, Garnet merely bowed slightly. Jeremy doffed his hat and walked over to his one-horse gig and got in. Turning, he bowed from the waist before taking up the reins and proceeding down the drive.

What an unusual encounter it had been, Garnet thought after Devlin had departed and she left for Cameron Hall a little later. Life was full of strange coincidences.

Garnet did not see Jeremy Devlin until after the closing ceremonies were over, and she was circulating among the parents and guests in the lovely restored gardens. She sensed he had been following her at some distance until the right opportunity presented itself for him to approach her.This time she was again surprised by his unexpected request to call upon her the next afternoon at Montclair.

Garnet was a little apprehensive about telling Sara, who was coming to call, and thankful that Clay was gone for a few days into Richmond.

At first, Sara pretended not to recall the incident and later in the day Garnet had to remind her she could not stay, because she was having company, and read to her until she fell asleep that afternoon.

''What company?'' Sara asked fretfully as Garnet brought her some herbal tea and helped her get settled for her afternoon nap.

''I told you, Mama. Remember that nice Major who

was so helpful to us, guarding the house and then bringing back Jonathan's pony? Remember, I told you his niece is one of our students?"

"Oh, that *Yankee!*" sniffed Sara disdainfully. "Garnet, I don't see how you can think of entertaining *one of them* after all they've done . . . my two darling boys gone, Malcolm forced to leave his birthplace, his heritage, and go God knows where? I can't stand to think of a Yankee under this roof . . . especially by *invitation!*"

Garnet left Sara and went to her own room to get ready for Jeremy. It had been such a long time since she had dressed to please a man's eyes, she thought half-mockingly as she surveyed herself in the mirror. She brushed her hair until it was smooth and shining, then pulled at the sides to make the little curls around her ears.

To her surprise Garnet found him to be delightful company, intelligent, interesting and an amusing raconteur as well. She discovered there was often a mischievous twinkle in those usually serious eyes. At one point she heard herself laugh at something he said, and realized with amazement that it had been a very long time since she had laughed.

He worked for a New York publishing firm and would be going to England in the fall to make contacts with some writers and publishers there.

"How wonderful," Garnet sighed. "I'm green with envy! I've never been to Europe—or anywhere for that matter." She gave a little shrug. "I've never been anywhere or done anything. I've spent my whole life within a radius of about sixty miles. Can you imagine?"

Jeremy Devlin studied her for a minute before replying, "But you're still so young! You have your whole life ahead of you—to travel, go places, do many things. . . ."

"Young? I feel a hundred years old." Garnet made a comic face, then laughed a little self-consciously. "And I suppose I'll spend the rest of my life right here, traveling back and forth between Montclair and Cameron Hall!"

"Not necessarily," Jeremy paused. "Is there any reason you should remain here instead of living with your mother at Cameron Hall?"

"My mother-in-law is an invalid and my father-in-law

173

. . . well, he just never has quite readjusted since the War . . . they both depend on me," she told, him wondering why she was confiding so much to this virtual stranger. But it seemed comfortable and natural.

"Things change, you know. Nothing ever stays exactly the same. The time may come when you feel you can leave," he said.

"If Malcolm came back . . ." Garnet began, then flushed. Jeremy looked puzzled, so she went on. "Malcolm is the oldest son, the heir. He was expected to take over the plantation, but—the War, and personal tragedies. . . ." She hesitated. "Afterward, he went West to California and until . . . I mean my *obligation* is *here*."

Garnet was glad of the interruption when Carrie brought out a tea tray to serve them on the veranda. There was no use in spilling out all her pent-up frustration about Malcolm to Jeremy.

"Cream or sugar, Mr. Devlin?" she asked.

"Just cream, and please, call me Jeremy?" his voice was tentative as if not sure he might not have overstepped the boundaries of their short acquaintance.

Jeremy Devlin called twice more before leaving Mayfield with his sister and niece, but not before he had asked Garnet if he could correspond with her during the summer.

When he rose to leave, she had given him her hand to say goodbye and he continued to hold it as he said, "If I should be able to come back to Virginia before sailing for England in September, may I call again?"

Although Garnet was tall, he towered over her and the pressure of his hand was firm on hers as she tried to withdraw it.

"Why yes, of course, Mr. Devlin, I should be pleased. . . ."

CHAPTER 2

SPRING TURNED INTO SUMMER and summer into early
autumn. A lovely haze hung over the hills and the sun
turned the yellow maples to gold. Along the drive the
giant elms formed an arch of russet and bronze and the
Virginia creeper blazed crimson as it clung to the sunny
side of the house.

On a beautiful September afternoon two letters were
delivered to Garnet at Montclair, and she took them out
to read them in the walled garden known as the English
Bride's garden.

The first was written in a bold, angular hand and she
knew almost before she opened it that it was from
Jeremy Devlin.

They had spent most of two delightful days together in
June after school closed. His sister had taken Malissa to
the Springs, but Jeremy had remained in Mayfield. He
had driven out each day to Montclair to visit Garnet.

Thinking of him now, Garnet read his letter with a
ripple of anticipation. He was accompanying his sister
and Malissa to Virginia when Cameron Hall opened, and
he was looking forward to coming to Montclair if she
could receive him.

Garnet felt her cheeks grow warm with pleasure as her
eyes skimmed again the line he had written: "I can

assure you it will be the high point of my trip, something I have been looking forward to since June."

As she read the letter through a second time, a mental picture of Jeremy Devlin came vividly to life. He was different from any man she had ever known. He had a quality of gentle strength combined with keen intelligence and an amusing wit. Although his manner was reserved, there was a special quality of warmth. She would be glad to see him again, she thought, as she refolded the letter and put it back in the envelope.

The second letter was a mystery. The envelope was of cheap paper written in a laboriously childish handwriting. When she opened it, she was surprised and touched.

"Dear Missy Garnet. Many times I have been wishing to rite to you but did not have the oppertunity. I have got two little chilren, a girl and a boy. The boy I named after Miss Rose's fine boy Jonathan James. James is after my husbin. The girl I named Lorena Rose. Lorena from the pretty song Miss Dove used to sing on the piano, do you remember? My husbin Jeems is working in the Mill here. I do laundry for some folks. We all doin well and in good health. Praise God. I larned to read more and now rite when my boy started school. We send our best love to you all. We hope all there is fine, too. TILDA"

For some reason tears came into Garnet's eyes as she finished reading this letter. How proud Rose would have been to see the results of all her efforts with Tilda. Obviously Tilda was still bettering herself, growing and learning.

One crisp fall morning not long afterward, Garnet was working in the garden, something she had discovered she loved to do. Trowel in hand, she was digging up bulbs to store for next spring's planting. The moist earth seemed to have a healing quality of its own. She had learned that during the War years when the vegetable garden had been a necessity and she had spent hours digging, hoeing, weeding, planting. In those days it had worked to lull the constant anxiety, dull the pain. Now she did it for the sheer joy.

Garnet was cutting the last of the chrysanthemums, tying up the stems, when a shadow fell across the ground from behind her and she sat back on her heels, looked up into Jeremy's handsome, smiling face.

"I didn't expect you so soon!" she gasped. "I never heard your carriage drive up!"

"I couldn't wait any longer to see you!" He held out his hands and helped her to her feet.

"But I'm hardly suitably dressed to receive company!" she said, looking down at the rough cotton pinafore she had on over an old calico dress with turned-up hem, and putting her hand to the battered straw hat tied under her chin with faded ribbons.

"You look beautiful to me!" Jeremy laughed but his eyes were serious.

Garnet felt flustered and quickly retorted, " 'Beauty is in the eye of the beholder,' they say, and *I* say you must be blind, Mr. Jeremy Devlin!"

He tucked her arm through his and they started walking along the garden path to the porch. There was something comforting in his solidness, his strength, and Garnet felt it as they strolled together. It had been so long since there had been a man's strength to lean against, she thought wistfully. It felt good. She had not realized how much she had missed that feeling. How she had denied needing it.

They sat down on the steps of the veranda where it circled the side of the house and was shaded by the leafy elms.

"I declare I should go do something about the way I look!" Garnet said, feeling self-conscious under his steady gaze. He put out a restraining hand.

"Don't! I meant it, you *do* look beautiful." He reached out and gently touched her cheek with the back of his hand, fingered a strand of hair her exertion and the heat of the sunny morning had dampened into curling tendrils. "I just want to look at you. I've thought of nothing else all summer."

Garnet was completely taken back by his frankness. All his former reserve seemed to have disappeared. He was looking at her in a way that gave her the strangest tingling sensation and she turned her head away. Her breath was quite fast and she suddenly did not know what to do with her hands.

177

"I'm sorry. Maybe, I shouldn't have said that. It's just that there is so little time. . . . I have only a day here before I have to leave for New York again and I sail for England on the fourteenth."

Garnet turned back to him in amazement.

"You mean you came all the way down here just . . ."

He finished it for her. "Just to see you. Yes. I thought I'd have longer, that I could lead up to what I want to say more gradually, more according to . . . traditional etiquette? But there was so much to do, so many arrangements to make that the time slipped by and I realized if I didn't come now, say what I wanted to say now, it would be months before I would see you again. I was afraid—" he broke off abruptly, Garnet was staring at him, lost in his words, silenced by their intensity.

The silence stretched between them for a long moment, then Jeremy said simply,

"I love you, Garnet."

"But . . . we hardly know each other!" she exclaimed.

"I feel as if I've known you forever. You've been in my heart and mind for a long time. I've carried an unforgettable picture of that beautiful, brave Southern lady for years. I could not get you out of my mind. You've haunted my waking hours and been in my dreams ever since the first time I saw you." He closed his eyes for a moment. "I can still see you, standing in the doorway in the moonlight. The porch was shadowy, and you held a candle in one hand, your hair all about your face . . . your lovely face with the light on it. . . ." He stopped. "Do I sound like a fool?"

She shook her head. "I don't know what to say."

"You don't have to say anything unless you want to. I guess I just had to tell you. I couldn't leave without telling you. Perhaps I rushed into this, perhaps I should have waited. . . . It hardly seems the right way but . . ." Another pause. "I had no real hope of ever seeing you again. Then, I did not know you were free."

He reached over and took her hand, gently removed her gardening glove, and raised it to his lips, kissed it.

"I would like to do so much for you, Garnet. I would like to love you, care for you, take you traveling, show you the world . . . give you the world. Do you think you could care for me . . . in time?"

Garnet was breathless, stunned by all Jeremy was saying. She jumped to her feet, his hand still holding hers. He stood too.

"I've frightened you, haven't I? I'm sorry." He sounded upset. "I've blundered when I wanted to be so careful. Have I ruined everything?"

Garnet shook her head, glad that the wide-brimmed hat hid her face. When at last she found her voice, the words tumbled out.

"Yes, I suppose I was frightened. I never thought, never guessed."

Long ago Garnet had lost her assurance that any man was hers for the application of a few flirtatious wiles. Life had been too difficult, too full of responsibilities during the last few years, to think anything would ever be different. Now, this stranger, this man of strength, intelligence, vigor, had come into a life she had come to accept and offered her a chance, a choice . . . the world!

"Then, you will think about what I've said? I may hope? While I'm away you'll have time to consider all the things . . . oh, Garnet, there is so much more I want to say. . . ."

Her voice softened, became a breath he had to bend to hear. "Yes, Jeremy."

"May I come again this evening?" he asked. "May we talk more later?"

She nodded.

"I do love you, Garnet," he said earnestly

She stood motionless as he left. She heard his boots crunching on the shell drive and she watched his tall figure mount and disappear down the drive.

He came earlier than expected and sheepishly apologized. "I found myself too restless."

Garnet, who had been ready and watching the drive for his arrival, smiled and led him into one of the two smaller parlors. There was a fire glowing in the marble fireplace. They sat on either side of the twin loveseats and, for a long moment, neither said anything, just watched the flames rising in red, blue, gold pyramids, while the

179

applewood logs snapped, scenting the room with pungent fragrance.

Finally it was Jeremy who spoke. He was watching the play of firelight on Garnet's face when he said, " Forgive me for staring. I'm trying to memorize you."

"You'll make me uneasy," she said but she smiled and handed him his tea.

"I want to engrave your features on my mind, for the picture must last such a long time. I wish we had time to have a photograph taken. You don't happen to have one, do you?"

Garnet thought of the unfinished portrait that was to hang along with the other Brides of Montclair in the hallway, and shook her head.

"No."

The room was still, with only the sound of the crackling fire on the hearth and the wind rising outside in the autumn evening to accompany the cadence of their beating hearts.

"Have you thought about what I said this morning, Garnet?" Jeremy asked gently after awhile.

"Yes, I have. And I should have told you right away, Jeremy, I am not *free*."

He sat forward in his chair, set down the teacup, clasped both hands in front of him, leaned toward her anxiously.

"You mean, there's someone else?"

Immediately Garnet thought of Malcolm. Had she really given up all hope of him? She was sure she had. Yet, should he suddenly come home, what then? But that was not what she meant when she had told Jeremy she wasn't free. How could she leave Montclair, abandon Sara and Clayton Montrose? They were so helpless, living out their days in a kind of relentless despair, reliving the days of glory that were gone and would never return. They were pitiable, but Garnet was bound by her pity for them.

Jeremy's intent gaze drew her and she had to look into his truth-probing eyes searching her very soul, delving into the secrets of her heart.

"Not in that way," she replied slowly, then tried to explain to him about the Montroses.

"I understand. But if you should marry, they would have to make the necessary adjustments, wouldn't they? Surely, they did not expect a young, vibrant, beautiful woman to remain a widow forever . . . to stay here with them?" Jeremy frowned.

"Five years ago I would never have imagined something like this happening. I never thought of marrying again—" *except to Malcolm,* Garnet had to add silently and truthfully.

"Five years ago we did not even know each other," Jeremy reminded her. "Now, everything is different."

Impulsively Garnet asked him. "Have you ever been in love?"

Jeremy smiled slightly. "Before now, you mean?"

She nodded.

"Yes. I was engaged to a lovely girl before the War. We'd known each other most of our lives. I did not think it fair to her to marry her, not knowing if I'd come back, or worse still, how I might come back. But she died. Consumption. She had always been delicate." His eyes were leveled at Garnet as he said, "We were both very young." He repeated, "Very young."

"I'm sorry. I did not mean to make you sad."

"You didn't. It's all part of my life just as your marriage, your loss is part of yours. Everything we go through becomes part of what we are. Sorrow either strengthens us or embitters us, don't you think?"

Garnet looked at him and felt his strong faith, his courage and optimism flowing through her. For the first time in years, she felt the stirring of hope. Maybe, after all, there was a new beginning possible. Before she could explore it further, Jeremy got up, came over, and knelt beside her. Their eyes were level. He cupped her chin with one hand and tilted her head so that they were only inches apart, and then he kissed her very tenderly.

She closed her eyes as he kissed her again, this time responding instinctively to the gentle insistence of his lips. Then, slowly the kiss ended and she opened her eyes again and dazedly looked into those deep-set loving ones.

In a strange way Garnet felt she had waited all her life for such a moment.

Later, they walked to the door, hand-in-hand. The time for parting had come.

"I will write as often as I can," Jeremy told her. "When I come back, perhaps you will know how you feel and whatever we need to do, we can do."

There was still so much unsettled, so much unresolved. This had all happened with such amazing swiftness Garnet's head reeled with it.

"I do love you. I know we can be happy together," Jeremy assured her.

Happy? Is happiness really attainable, to me, to anyone? Once she might have believed in the "happily ever after" of fairy tales. But she had been stripped of romantic illusions by the reality of her life. She wasn't sure she believed in happiness any more.

That night Garnet stood at her bedroom window and gazed out at a scene she had looked at a thousand times. But this night had a dreamlike quality. Montclair and its surroundings were wrapped in a kind of magical light, the moon shimmering down through the trees, enveloping everything in an unbroken peace.

She knew a life with someone like Jeremy would be entirely different from anything she had known before. He was Northern-born, bred, educated. He was cultured, well-traveled, worldly, urbane, sophisticated. He was also mature, considerate, gentle. A different kind of man from her experience.

She had been married to a boy—Bryce of the boyish charm, the sweet, easy-going manner. He had loved her in his fashion and, in the end, she had cared deeply for him.

She had hero-worshiped Malcolm, dreamed about him, imagined and fantasized a romance. But now she realized she had never really loved nor been loved by any man.

Jeremy Devlin was offering her just that, a second chance at life, a second chance for love, the possibility of a new kind of happiness. And when he returned from England, he would demand her answer.

Garnet turned away from the window, took off her robe, and got into bed. But an hour later, by the striking of the big Grandfather clock downstairs, she was still wide awake.

Maybe it was the moonlight streaming in the window that was keeping her awake . . . maybe. She moved restlessly, shifting her body so that the milky glow of moonlight would not be in her eyes. Why was she sleepless after such a long, eventful day? Was it just the moonlight? Or was it the disturbing thoughts of Jeremy Devlin?

He loved her, she thought in some wonder. Perhaps he had first fallen in love with an imaginary woman, a vision held in a romantic, misty dream, but now he must see something in her that attracted, compelled.

But did she love him? Enough to marry him? Garnet knew she would have to find the answer in her own heart.

CHAPTER 3

TRULY THE MONTHS that followed were drably monotonous. She had a great deal of responsibility at both Montclair and Cameron Hall, and sometimes felt overwhelmed by the problems of both households of which she was a part.

Cameron Hall was in a sad state of disrepair, and even the high fees paid by the boarding students barely covered the expenses of feeding them, heating the cavernous rooms and paying taxes.

It was worse at Montclair. What few servants remained were old and feeble. Trained as house servants, they were unwilling to do the tasks relegated to field hands in former days. The roof leaked; the chimneys glutted with resin and choked with rain-soaked leaves caused the fireplaces to smoke, and there was no one to chop firewood to keep the house warm.

Sara had never grown accustomed to the lack of luxury and complained more and more bitterly as she moved into old age. Mr. Montrose had become vague and crochety and spent most of his time playing chess by himself or staring vacantly out the windows onto the bleak landscape.

The only bright spots in the long, dreary winter were Jeremy's letters that arrived regularly, sometimes as often as twice a week, filled with vivid descriptions of the places he was visiting, the people he was meeting, the interesting events he was attending in a world far from the isolated one at Montclair. In each one he reminded her of the answer she had promised to give him when he came to Mayfield in the spring.

Garnet spent much time thinking and praying about that answer. She admired Jeremy, had come to appreciate his consideration, his sensitivity and intelligence—but did she love him?

Since Bryce, Garnet was very much aware of her failure as a wife. She did not want to make the mistake of marrying a man she could not love the way a husband should be cherished. The question that nagged her most—was she worthy of Jeremy?

As Sara became more querulous, Garnet saw her own selfishness reflected in the older woman. As she practiced patience in dealing with her mother-in-law, she was convicted by the lack of it. She thought she had changed, but had she really? Maybe not.

But Garnet was wrong about herself. She could not see what others now saw in her face—the character and courage, the strength and determination. She carried her slender body with a pride that was not arrogant, yet gave the impression of confidence. She had a new beauty and dignity. All she had been through had altered her on a deeper level. Her view of life had changed, had made her more aware of people, given her the ability to feel more—both joy and pain.

The winter months crawled by one after the other while Garnet ached desperately for spring. Sometimes she wondered if the parade of gray days would ever end.

Then suddenly in the middle of March, spring burst forth, almost overnight. Montclair sprang to life. Pink and white dogwood, the deep magentas of rhododendrons, the delicate pinks of azaleas, carpets of yellow jonquils and blue and lavender iris, rows of tulips in all colors brightened Garnet's heart and lifted her spirit.

One day she brought in armfuls of daffodils and was arranging them in vases to take up to Sara's room. So absorbed was she in her task that she heard nothing until she heard her name spoken.

"Garnet?"

At first she was paralyzed by the familiarity of the voice and her instant recognition of it. Then common sense corrected that. *It couldn't be! Could it?* The flowers she was holding dropped from her hands and slowly she turned.

The man's figure filling the pantry doorway blotted out the sunlight, and his face was in the shadow. But there was no mistaking his identity.

Garnet's throat went dry, her heart suddenly seemed not her own but some wild thing beating in her breast as her lips formed his name soundlessly.

He spoke again. "You look like you've seen a ghost," and there was that old teasing quality in his voice.

"Malcolm. Malcolm, is it really you?" she asked weakly, wiping her damp hands on her apron. She took two steps toward him then stopped.

"Yes, Garnet. It is. I've come home."

He came over to her and all at once all the years in between flew away. She held out her arms and he caught her up in a hug that lifted her off her feet.

A tumultuous mix of emotions exploded in Garnet as her arms went around him, felt his tighten around her. The old childhood devotion, the adoring unconditional love, the ecstatic relief of having him in the flesh, being able to touch, feel and hold him caused in her a crazy euphoria. Malcolm was home at last! At last there would be someone to share all the burdens, someone who would know what to do, who would take the lead. Garnet leaned against him half-sobbing, half-laughing, saying his name over and over.

Then she felt his arms loosen and an imperceptible stiffening of his body as he gradually disengaged himself from her embrace.

Garnet swayed slightly as he released her, and she put her hand out behind her to steady herself against the edge of the table.

It was only then she saw the girl standing in the doorway behind Malcolm. Garnet looked at her then back at Malcolm in bewilderment. His eyes seemed gray and very cold.

He turned, and with a sweeping flourish of his hat,

said, "Garnet, may I present my wife, Blythe, and this is my *sister-in-law*—Garnet Cameron—*Montrose*."

The girl took a timid step into the kitchen, glancing at Malcolm as if for permission to advance further.

Garnet's knees went weak all at once, and she sat down in one of the kitchen chairs. The girl's beauty stunned her. She was tall and her voluptuous curves gave her an almost bold appearance, if it were not for the innocence of her wide eyes, the childlike look of eagerness for approval. She was peculiarly dressed, Garnet thought, in a dress of satin with deep lapels and cuffs from which the trimming seemed to have been removed. Her bonnet, too, seemed shiny and of new material but was curiously lacking in adornment such as one would expect.

After that strangely impersonal impression, Garnet was conscious of the merciless knife of pain twisting inside her, as her mind absorbed Malcolm's introduction.

Her gaze turned to Malcolm, the cherished familiar figure who had become this cold stranger. Where he had been slender and graceful of build, he was broader of shoulder and lean. His eyes were curiously guarded and the full beard and mustache disguised the face she had loved so long and knew so well.

Drawing a deep breath that cut into her chest painfully as if jagged shards of glass were breaking within her, Garnet at last managed to ask, "But why didn't you write? Let us know—"

"It would have been too much to explain. I wasn't sure how long it would take to get to you. I thought we would arrive before a letter. . . ." He paused. "How is my mother?"

Garnet stared at him incredulously. What was Malcolm saying? Married? He had *married* this—this girl? While she had struggled here alone, keeping his child, nursing his mother, running this place, all by herself? Expending every ounce of her strength to keep Montclair, for him! She had neglected her own family . . . she could have gone to Cameron Hall, been with her own mother . . . but she had stayed here. For him!

With great effort Garnet rose from the chair, holding

on to the table's edge with a white-knuckled hand, commanding every nerve in her body to stop quivering.

"I'll have to prepare her. This will be—somewhat of a shock. If you will excuse me—" she nodded to Blythe, unable to do more. Then moving with what she hoped was dignity, she passed them where they stood and walked out of the kitchen into the hall. At the foot of the staircase, she leaned on it for a moment, her breath coming shallowly. Praying for strength and with a valiant calling up of will power, she mounted the steps. She held herself tightly, thin shoulders straight, until she reached the second balcony, then she lifted her skirts and ran down the hall to her room.

There she flung herself upon her knees beside her bed, pleading for help.

"God! My God!" was all she could utter as anguish flooded over her. Malcolm was home—and he had brought a bride—again! All the old pain of that long-ago day when he had brought Rose to Montclair assailed her, and yet—it was not the same.

Gradually Garnet stopped shaking. She became very still as if listening. In a few minutes a calm, almost a peace began to steal over her. What was it Tilda had said when she left Montclair to find a new life? She had repeated something learned from Rose: "Ye shall know the Truth and the Truth shall set you free."

Garnet struggled with the truth. Malcolm had never loved her the way she wanted him to—she would have to finally accept that. Now he was forever out of reach. It was so final she could feel the raw hurt of it like a piece of fine porcelain broken beyond repair.

The shock of Malcolm's homecoming, the fact that he had brought home a bride, was devastating. But with it there was also a feeling of relinquishment that was almost good, peaceful.

She could leave Montclair now. There would be a new mistress here and Malcolm would take over the care of his parents, the responsibilities that were now his.

Garnet could leave with no recriminations, no regrets. There was a future to think about. A future, perhaps, with Jeremy Devlin. At any rate, she could go freely, leaving the past behind.

Garnet gathered her pride around her like a ragged cloak, and got up from her knees. She would tell Sara of Malcolm's return, then she would go downstairs and welcome the new mistress properly.

CHAPTER 4

GARNET WAS BACK in the room she had slept in as a child at Cameron Hall. She had left it to become the bride of Bryce Montrose over ten years ago. Now, it was as though she had come full circle.

Within days of Malcolm's return, Garnet had left Montclair. She had left without looking back. She knew it would take time to sort through all the emotions she felt. A good part of her life had been spent at Montclair, an important part, and now she had to begin a new one.

It was late spring and Garnet was awaiting Jeremy Devlin's return. He had written from New York after docking, telling her that he would leave for Virginia in a few days and would come to Cameron Hall as soon as he arrived.

Garnet's feelings were divided—she was both eager and reluctant to see him. Jeremy was coming for the answer she had promised him. It had been almost a year since she had given him that promise. Now she felt uncertain, unsure.

She had dressed carefully in a dress Dove had altered beautifully for her from a pre-War gown. Though the material was still good, it would probably look terribly out of style to Jeremy, who, by now, was accustomed to seeing ladies wearing the fashionable gowns of London and Paris. She was giving a final pat to her hair when she heard the sound of carriage wheels on the drive below her bedroom window. Clasping her hands tightly together, she resisted peeking out to see Jeremy mount the terrace steps.

She held her breath, hearing the murmur of voices downstairs, until there was a light knock at the door, and Dove, smiling, peered around the edge of the door, whispered, "Mr. Devlin is here, Garnet. And, my, but he looks splendid!"

Descending the stairway Garnet could see into the drawing room. Jeremy was standing in front of the fireplace and, as she reached the last step, he looked into the mirror and caught her reflection. Garnet halted, pausing, with one hand on the banister rail, as their eyes met. She drew in her breath and felt a sensation, both new and exciting, tremor through her. As the moment lengthened she felt a tremendous warmth flowing all over her and her heart began to pound.

Slowly Jeremy turned as she took that last step. Striding forward, he waited as she crossed the hall to meet him.

There was, after all, no need for words. The question was already in his eyes. She stood a few feet from him. "Well?" he said.

Garnet looked up into the face, beyond the handsome features, and met that loving gaze. Once and for all, she knew what her answer would be. Suddenly all the doubts, the old sorrows and disillusionments were swept away. She felt young again, deliriously happy.

"Yes!" she whispered huskily.

"Yes?" he repeated as if he had not quite heard correctly. "Yes, you will marry me?"

Garnet nodded solemnly. "Yes, Jeremy."

"Oh, my darling Garnet . . . I'm so . . ." for once the articulate, suave Jeremy seemed at a loss for words. Instead, he opened his arms and Garnet walked into them. As they closed around her Garnet felt serenely happy, sheltered and at peace.

As she heard him murmur her name, his hand smoothing her hair, she sighed contentedly, leaned against him. It was as if the icy hardness that had formed around the

191

softness of her heart to ward off hurt suddenly melted and she was flooded with joy. The lovely words of the beautiful Song of Solomon she had learned sang in her spirit:

For, lo, the winter is past,
The rain is over and gone;
The flowers appear on the earth;
The time of the singing of birds is come. . . .

EN ROUTE TO ENGLAND

1870

Faith, hope, love . . . and the greatest of these is love.
1 Corinthians 13:13

THE HUGE STEAMSHIP moved slowly out of New York Harbor. Standing at its rail, a graceful woman in amethyst velvet traveling suit and mink capelet turned and smiled at the tall, dark-haired man at her side.

"I can hardly believe it! It's like a fairy tale. I'm really on my way to England!"

"And Paris! Then Italy and Switzerland!" The look he gave her was so tender and loving it made her feel undeserving. "I want to take you everywhere, show you everything!" He took her hand in his and asked her earnestly, "Did I tell you how enormously happy you've made me?"

Jeremy raised her hand to his lips, then singled out the third finger of her left hand where beside the gold wedding band was the cluster of garnets and diamonds he had brought her from Austria for her engagement ring.

Garnet did not say anything, but the light in those beautiful amber eyes spoke volumes. She still found it hard to express to Jeremy how much she loved him.

Garnet, who had thought she would never know happiness, had decided if she could find contentment, that would be enough. She had never expected to know the thrill of a man's touch, the sweet taste of desire, the surging response to passion or the deep fulfillment of complete love. But she had found them all in Jeremy.

Garnet who thought she had lost everything, had been given her heart's desire. Just as the prophet Joel had predicted: "I will restore the years the locusts have eaten."

They stood together watching the shoreline grow dimmer and more distant. Virginia, Montclair seemed very far away now. But Garnet knew a new life waited for her just beyond that far horizon.

"Come, darling, it's getting cold," Jeremy whispered. "Let's go in."

Garnet slipped her hand into his and they walked toward the opening door ahead.

ABOUT THE AUTHOR

A native of North Carolina, JANE PEART is deeply rooted in her beloved Southland, a fact that gives color and credence to the poignant stories she has crafted for the series, "The Brides of Montclair." The third in this multivolume saga, REBEL BRIDE is perhaps her most ambitious and touching work.

A prolific writer, Jane has published widely and is featured in the text, WRITING ROMANCE FICTION FOR LOVE AND MONEY, by Helene Schellenberg Barnhart. a publication of Writers Digest Books. In addition, she is a frequent speaker at writers conferences throughout the country.

Jane currently resides with her husband in Eureka, California. They are the parents of two grown daughters who share their enthusiasm for the arts.

A Letter To Our Readers

Dear Reader:

Pioneering is an exhilarating experience, filled with opportunities for exploring new frontiers. The Zondervan Corporation is proud to be the first major publisher to launch a series of inspirational romances designed to inspire and uplift as well as to provide wholesome entertainment. In order that we might better contribute to your reading enjoyment, we would appreciate your taking a few minutes to respond to the following questions and return to:

> Anne Severance, Editor
> Zondervan Publishing House
> 1415 Lake Drive
> Grand Rapids, Michigan   49506

1. Did you enjoy reading REBEL BRIDE?
   - ☐ Very much. I would like to see more books by this author!
   - ☐ Moderately
   - ☐ I would have enjoyed it more if _____

2. Where did you purchase this book? _____

3. What influenced your decision to purchase this book?
   - ☐ Cover
   - ☐ Title
   - ☐ Publicity
   - ☐ Back cover copy
   - ☐ Friends
   - ☐ Other _____

4. Please rate the following elements from 1 (poor) to 10 (superior).

- [ ] Heroine
- [ ] Hero
- [ ] Setting
- [ ] Plot
- [ ] Inspirational theme
- [ ] Secondary characters

5. Which settings would you like to see in future Serenade/Saga Books?

_____ _____

_____ _____

6. What are some inspirational themes you would like to see treated in future books?

_____ _____

_____ _____

7. Would you be interested in reading other Serenade/Serenata or Serenade/Saga Books?

- [ ] Very interested
- [ ] Moderately interested
- [ ] Not interested

8. Please indicate your age range:

- [ ] Under 18
- [ ] 18–24
- [ ] 25–34
- [ ] 35–45
- [ ] 46–55
- [ ] Over 55

9. Would you be interested in a Serenade book club? If so, please give us your name and address:

Name _____

Occupation _____

Address _____

City _____ State _____ Zip _____

Serenade/Saga Books are inspirational romances in historical settings, designed to bring you a joyful, heart-lifting reading experience.

Serenade/Saga books now available in your local bookstore:

Watch for these Serenade Books in the coming months: